THE BRIDE
WORE COVERALLS

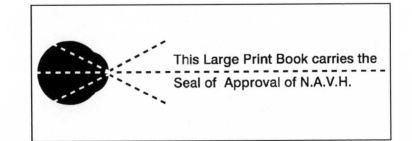

This Large Print Book carries the
Seal of Approval of N.A.V.H.

THE BRIDE WORE COVERALLS

DEBRA ULLRICK

THORNDIKE PRESS

A part of Gale, Cengage Learning

Detroit • New York • San Francisco • New Haven, Conn • Waterville, Maine • London

GALE
CENGAGE Learning™

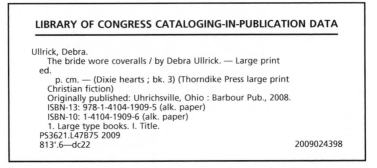

LIBRARY OF CONGRESS CATALOGING-IN-PUBLICATION DATA

Ullrick, Debra.
The bride wore coveralls / by Debra Ullrick. — Large print ed.
   p. cm. — (Dixie hearts ; bk. 3) (Thorndike Press large print Christian fiction)
   Originally published: Uhrichsville, Ohio : Barbour Pub., 2008.
   ISBN-13: 978-1-4104-1909-5 (alk. paper)
   ISBN-10: 1-4104-1909-6 (alk. paper)
   1. Large type books. I. Title.
PS3621.L47B75 2009
813'.6—dc22   2009024398

Published in 2009 by arrangement with Barbour Publishing, Inc.

Printed in Mexico
1 2 3 4 5 6 7 13 12 11 10 09

DEDICATION

In memory of my beloved sister-in-law, Linda Elaine Suppes (1951–2006). I love you and miss you terribly.

Joe, Amanda, Jaydon, Brent, Chrissie, Leah, and Beau Suppes, I love you all very much.

A ginormous thanks to my extraordinary friend/mentor/tutor, Staci Stallings — you and Jesus helped make this happen. Jeanne Leach and Michelle Sutton, thanks for believing in me. Terri Smith in Alabama, Joe Docheff, and ACFW members — thanks for all your help. Sharmane Wikberg, look what you started. Mom loves you, kiddo. Rick Ullrick, I love you more than words can say. Thanks for believing in me and supporting me. You're *my* hero.

CHAPTER 1

"As much as I hate to say it, their chauvinistic remarks are starting to get me down," Camara Cole admitted to her best friend, Lolly Morrison.

"Ca-mare-ah Che-velle Cole," Lolly said in an exaggerated pronunciation of her name, "don't you dare let them pull you down." Lolly shook her well-manicured finger at her. "Stan teases you, too, and he's proud of your accomplishments."

Camara searched her friend's eyes to see if she was just trying to make her feel better. "Is he really?"

"Yes. He tells me that all the time. In fact . . ." Lolly's red curls bounced as she glanced around Tooties Gourmet Coffee Shop. Camara followed her gaze, wondering what she was looking for. "Yesterday Stan told me he wished he was as good at building and racing mud bog trucks as you are."

Shock rippled through her. "Stan?" She

dipped her head sideways. "We're talking about your husband Stan, right?"

Lolly laughed. "Yes. I'm talking about my Stan. What other Stan do you know?"

Camara shook her head. "He really said that?"

Lolly put her coffee cup down and laid her hand on top of Camara's. "How long have you known me, Cam? Would I lie to you?"

"No. But it's just hard to believe. Stan teases me almost as much as the rest of the guys."

Lolly flipped her wrist. "Oh, you know how guys are. They stick together. By the way," she said as she shook her finger at Camara, "don't you go telling Stan I told you what he said. He'll never tell me anything again."

"I won't." Camara smiled. She picked up her drink and took a sip. "It's all Chase Lamar's fault. Ever since *I*" — Camara tapped her chest — "a mere female, started beating his times, Chase has said women have no business racing in a *man's sport*." Camara rolled her eyes. "The frustrating part about this whole thing is now he has the rest of the guys teasin' me, too. I get so angry anymore. I've prayed about my temper, and I'm trying to get it under control, but man, those guys sure know how to goad me." She tucked her shoulder-length blond hair behind her ears. "Honestly, Loll . . . I don't know what to do. Last Saturday at Pete's Mud-n-Track, they were horrible. Especially Bobby-Rae."

"What did Bobby-Rae do?"

"Well, when I finished checking under the hood of The Black Beast, Bobby-Rae came up and started saying all sorts of cruel things."

"Like what?"

Camara pursed her face to imitate Bobby-Rae's macho attitude and quoted him. " 'You're a disgrace to Southern women. Women don't race, and women don't build trucks. When ya gonna quit playin' mechanic and act like a real lady?' " Camara shook her head. "I refuse to live in a time warp. Besides, I know Bobby-Rae's just mad because I refused to go out with him. I —"

"Bobby-Rae asked you out?" Lolly's blue eyes widened. When Camara didn't deny it, Lolly raised her eyebrows. "Well, shoot a monkey and kiss a pig. I can't believe it. When?"

"After work one night a few weeks ago."

"What did you say?"

"I told him no. That it was nothing personal, but I'd made it a rule a long time ago never to date coworkers because too many times it causes problems on the job. And, boy, has it."

"Well, that explains his attitude toward you. Is that all he said?"

"After I turned him down, he went on and on about how greasy my fingernails and hair were." Camara held her hands out. Studying her rough-looking hands and chipped nails, she inwardly cringed. "I know my nails are a mess. But what'd he expect? I'm a mechanic. Besides, he didn't have to say it the way he did. It really hurt."

"So that's why you changed your hair-style?"

Camara self-consciously touched her hair. "Yeah, I thought maybe if I looked more feminine, the guys would leave me alone. I've never worn bangs before. Does it look okay?"

"I love it. It makes your eyes look bigger. I wish I had pretty brown eyes like yours." She popped a bite of raspberry-swirl cake into her mouth. "But enough of that. Did he say anything else?"

"No, not that night. But he started ripping on me again at Pete's Mud-n-Track last Saturday. He repeated everything he'd said the night I turned him down. Plus he said" — she pulled her face into a manly pose to imitate Bobby-Rae again — " 'No man in his right mind would ever go out with a Miss Know-It-All like you.' " Camara chuckled.

Lolly's brows rose. "What's funny about that?"

"Nothing. That's not why I'm laughing. You won't believe what happened next." Camara snitched a small piece of Lolly's cake and tossed it in her mouth. "Guess who came to my rescue?"

"Who?"

"Take a guess."

"Your brother, Erik?"

"Nope. Chase Lamar, that's who."

Lolly's mouth dropped open so fast Camara giggled.

"Well, I'll be. You're kidding, right?" Lolly blinked several times.

"Nope. I about passed out from shock."

Lolly slowly shook her head. "That's a hard one to believe."

"I know. Ironic, isn't it?"

"Y'all have been rivals for as long as I can remember," Lolly said. "He's teased you unmercifully for years." Lolly moved her coffee out of the way and leaned toward Camara. "I want to know everything. And don't leave anything out."

"Not a whole lot to tell. Chase told him,

11

'Leave her alone, Bobby-Rae. And apologize to the lady.' Bobby-Rae opened his mouth, but Erik showed up and Bobby-Rae hustled to his truck and hightailed it out of Pete's Mud-n-Track like his backside was on fire."

"And?"

"And nothing. Erik and Chase started talking, and I went back to work on my bog truck." Camara took a long drink of her coffee. "I still can't believe Chase and Erik are good friends now. Maybe Erik felt sorry for Chase because the first couple of times Chase came to singles night at church he looked pretty uncomfortable. Erik always does gravitate toward those in need of help. And Chase *definitely* needs plenty of help." She snickered then turned serious. "Ya know, Loll, ever since John started bringing Chase to singles night at church, he doesn't act like the same obnoxious bully. He's . . . well, he's almost sweet."

"That *has* to be God."

They both laughed.

While finishing their coffee, they chatted about some of the drastic changes in Chase.

For years Camara and Chase had been Chevy/Ford rivals. Just like their parents. Except his dad used family money to purchase Ford dealerships, and her dad, through hard work and perseverance, bought Chevrolet dealerships. But the real rivalry began when they both started mud bog racing four years ago. Chase had become downright ornery and sometimes cruel. And now he was . . . what was he? Camara decided she didn't know or care. She didn't want to think about Chase Lamar.

As much as Camara hated to leave her friend's company, she picked up the keys to her Hummer and stuck them in the pocket of her faded jeans. "Well, Loll, I'd better go. I have a few vehicles at the shop I need to work on the next couple of days, plus I want to finish getting The Black Beast ready for Saturday's mud bog race."

Outside, Camara shielded her eyes against April's warm sun and glanced at the row of historical buildings lining the streets of Swamper City, Alabama. They reminded her of the men she raced with . . . out-of-date and antiquated. In the past when she raced at several other places in the Heart of Dixie, none of the men were offended that she raced bog trucks and was a mechanic. In fact, they were just as friendly and hospitable as the rest of the people in Alabama. Camara heaved a sigh, jumped in her Hummer, and drove toward Cole's Chevrolet. Maybe it was something in Swamper City's water that made the men here act the way they did. Camara laughed at that thought. It was a possibility.

At four thirty the next morning, Camara pulled into Cole's Chevrolet and parked. She loved getting to work early. That way she got all her work done during the week so she could race on Saturdays. She hustled into the auto shop and headed straight to her work stall.

Awed by the 1958 Corvette parked in front of her, Camara lovingly ran her fingers over the baby blue classic. She hurried into her yellow grease-stained coveralls and opened the hood. Goose bumps rose on her arms. What a privilege to work on Mr. Banks's pride and joy. She still couldn't believe he trusted its care to her only. Well, she wouldn't let him down. She'd have it fixed in no time.

Three hours later the Corvette roared to life. Satisfied with a job well done, Camara leaned over to pick up her tools. Footsteps sounded behind her. Smiling, she stood and turned. Her smile dropped at the sight of a big burly man. He may have been handsome, but his hairy body and tattoos reminded her of a rebel biker. Good thing she'd made the no-dating-coworkers rule a

14

long time ago. He was definitely not her type. "What are you doing here so early?"

Bobby-Rae's gray eyes darkened. "I came to see if I could work on Mr. Banks's car. But, as usual, the boss's daughter gets to."

Camara frowned. "What does me being the boss's daughter have to do with anything?"

He snorted. "Well, it definitely ain't because you're a better mechanic than the rest of us here, that's for sure. No man in his right mind would ask a *woman*" — he spat out the term as if it were a dirty word — "to work on a vehicle of this quality unless he was insane or, in this case, a friend of the family."

Camara shook her head. It wasn't just Mr. Banks who requested her. Several people did, and each time it angered the men she worked with. So what was she supposed to do? Not do a good job so their egos were pacified? No way. She had worked hard to get where she was. If the men she worked with couldn't handle that people requested her, then that was their problem. Not wanting to defend herself for the millionth time, she tossed out the only word she could think of. "Jealous." She brushed past him and headed toward the restroom.

■ ■ ■ ■

Saturday proved to be a nice sunny day. Camara stood at the front of the mud pit at the east end of Swamper Speedway's oval racetrack. The foamy water on top of the mire reminded her of froth on a root beer float — or a black cow, as her mamaw would call it. She glanced at the empty wooden grandstands that covered one side of the racetrack, knowing that in a couple of hours they would be full of spectators.

The sound of loud glasspack mufflers drew her attention. Two pickups pulling trailers entered the contestant's area. Pretty snazzy — and pricey. Camara looked around at the few other rigs that were there. She recognized several of them and marveled at what she saw. Knowing what some of them did for a living, they surely must have gone into hock to own those rigs. Camara gave a short snort. Typical of most people who love vehicles and racing — they would rather have a garage full of cars, pickups, and monster trucks than eat. Well, okay, maybe not eat, but close. Camara wasn't any different. Except that hers were paid for. However, if she had had enough room in her garage, she'd own a variety of classic cars and trucks with big tires and lift kits. As it stood now, she had a Hummer, which she bought at cost through her dad's dealership, a '68 Camaro that her dad gave her on her eighteenth birthday — he was the original owner — and her '74 Chevy bog truck that she picked up at a junkyard for a hundred dollars and completely modified.

Looking up, Camara did a double take at the bog vehicle pulling in. Sitting high on a trailer, the bogger resembled a giant outer space bug. She wondered what it sounded like and how it ran. From the looks of the other contestants' vehicles, she might have some stiff competition today. She turned her attention to the 3 1/2-foot-deep, 150-foot-long mud pits to see if today was one of those days when they added more mud to the usual twenty inches. Sometimes they did that, and it made a real difference to anyone who wanted to win.

"Don't fret your pretty little head off." Chase's deep Southern drawl boomed from behind her. "With any luck, your poor Chevy will make it through."

Startled, Camara sucked in a sharp breath and spun around. Her foot slipped on the clay mud. One leg headed directly toward the mud pit, which was exactly where the rest of her would have followed if not for

Chase's strong arm encircling her, hauling her upright.

The rain-fresh scent of his aftershave wafted up her nose, reminding her of a spring shower. As he steadied her, she gazed into his dark green eyes, mere inches from her face. She knew she should exercise her manners and thank him, but she didn't. It was his fault in the first place that she'd been nearly dipped in mud.

She moved away from him so he was between her and the pits. "Do you always sneak up on people?" she asked frostily, her heart rapping at two thousand rpms. Planting her hands on her hips, she sent him an icy stare.

Chase chuckled. "By the way, *Camaro,* you're welcome."

"It's *Ca-mare-ah,* thank you very much. And I'm welcome for what?" She tipped her head sideways and hiked a brow.

"For saving ya from an unwanted mud bath." He grinned.

She clenched her jaw. That man could be so infuriating. She was in no humor to play his game — whatever it was. Instead she wanted to wipe that smug grin right off his face. Strutting close to him, she shook her finger under his nose. "What do ya mean you rescued me? *You're* the reason I almost fell in the first place, sneaking up on me like that."

"I didn't sneak up on you. You were just concentrating too hard." Squinting, he rubbed his chin. "Afraid your truck won't make it through, huh?"

Camara glared up at him from shoulder level.

Chase's eyes twinkled. "Anyway, ya owe me."

"What do you mean, I owe you? Owe you for what?"

A deep chuckle rumbled from Chase's throat.

Camara pursed her mouth and frowned. Was he laughing at her — again? Her anger started boiling over like an overheated radiator. She jutted her chin and spun the bill of her yellow Chevy cap around. *One, two, three. Help me to control my anger, Lord. Four . . .*

"Ya owe me because as tiny as you are, if you'd have fallen in that pit, no one would be able to find ya."

Five, six . . . I'm trying, Lord.

"So, see, I just saved ya from a muddy grave." His snide grin did it.

"Ack! You!" She shoved him hard.

Eyes widening, Chase backpedaled and his arms flailed as he futilely tried to avoid

19

falling into the trench. Camara couldn't hold down the laughter bubbling from within as he landed with a *smack* in the thick mud.

Quick as a flash Chase jumped to his feet, but he lost his balance. Struggling to stay upright in the knee-high mud, he staggered before falling forward. He shot his arms in front of him to break his fall but plunged face-first deeply into the mud. When he finally stood again, his body was coated with muck, and a shock-filled gaze peered out from under his mud-masked face. His normally spiked dark brown hair lay limp from the heavy mire.

"That'll teach ya," she declared, pivoting in triumph.

She'd barely taken a step when muddy arms wrapped around her waist, tugging her backward. Her Chevy cap flipped off her head and landed on the ground.

"Noo!" Camara screamed, but it was too late.

Chase pulled her down next to him in the pit. She gasped at the gooey mud. Using Chase for leverage, she stood. Her mouth fell open. Even in the shallowest part of the mud pit she couldn't see her knees. She shook her hands, trying to rid them of the gelatinous mud that was starting to seep through her shoes and clothes.

"That'll teach me what?" Chase snorted with a mixture of indignation and humor.

Insufferable man! Camara scooped up a big glob of mud, her mouth curved in a vengeful smile. Twisting without warning, she slung it at him, hitting him square in the mouth. Chase sputtered and spat.

Now was her chance to escape. In hopes that her tennis shoes remained on her feet, Camara gripped them with her toes and leaned forward toward the embankment. Using her arms to balance herself, she forced one leg forward and then the next. One more step and she'd be able to climb out.

Suddenly she felt solid arms wrap around her, pulling her backward.

"Oh no, ya don't. You're not getting away that easy, *Ca-mare-O.*" Pulling her back tight against his chest, Chase pinned her arms to her body and scooped up a handful of mud with his free hand.

"Don't you dare!" She fought to twist sideways, rearing her head and staring up defiantly at him.

"Or what?"

His hand headed toward her face. She jerked her head back and forth, but Chase managed to smear her cheeks and chin with mud. Camara strained to free herself from his strong but strangely gentle grasp. However, Chase held her even closer to his chest.

"Ya know, Cammy," — he waggled his eyebrows — "in Hollywood they pay a fortune for this stuff. So, see, I'm doing your skin a huge favor, and it didn't cost ya one red cent." He tossed back his head and roared with laughter.

Camara dipped a handful of mud, flung her hand behind her, and slapped it against his neck.

"So, that's how ya wanna play, huh?" His voice sounded mischievous.

In one fluid motion he gathered a large handful of mud, held it over Camara's head, and shot her a wicked grin.

As much as she hated to admit even to herself, she was enjoying this playful side of Chase. She ducked when a few clumps landed in her hair.

"You play dirty." She tried wiggling out of his grasp. "No fair. You're stronger than me."

Chase drew her closer and waved the mud mere inches from her face. "Do you concede defeat then, matey?" he asked in a pirate accent.

"Never, vermin! I shall go down with the ship first," she imitated him. The mud was a whisper away from her mouth. She arched her head backward. "Let me put it to you this way. If you do, I'll just have to pay you back." She smirked and then smiled sweetly.

He leaned his head down. His breath brushed across her face when he spoke, "Oh yeah, and just *how* will you pay me back?" His eyes twinkled and then turned serious when he glanced at her lips.

Camara swallowed hard. She didn't like the look on his face. Was he going to try and kiss her? Well, there was no way she'd let Chase Lamar kiss her, no matter how good-looking he was. She jerked herself free and scrambled out of the pit.

Snatching up her cap, she stoically made her way toward her vehicle. The muddy clothes clung to her, making it difficult to walk.

Chase strolled up beside her. "If your Chevy moved half as fast as you did just now in that pit, ya just might have a chance of winning today. But don't count on it. It's a Chevy." He chuckled.

Camara stopped dead in her tracks. She turned sideways, facing him.

"My Chevy moves just fine, thank you very much. It's that Ford of yours ya need to be concerned with." Placing her finger over her lips, she squinted. "Hmm. Now

23

let's see . . . what does Ford stand for again?" She snapped her muddy fingers. "Oh yeah, I remember: Fix Or Repair Daily. Or, Found On the Road Dead. Too bad there aren't any initials for 'Can't run worth diddly-squat.' " She sent him a smug grin.

Truth be known, she liked Fords, Dodges, and just about any other make of vehicle. She liked their power and the intense challenges they presented. But she'd keep that information tucked away from Chase or anyone else.

"No, Ford stands for: First On Race Day." He grinned. "Remember last week? It was *my* Ford that beat *your* Chevy."

"And do you remember the week before that? It was *my* Chevy that won the *big* trophy and the *big* moneys at Jenson's Speedway," Camara stated proudly. "And I seem to recall you telling me that me and my Chevy had zero chance of winning." She smiled smugly.

"You still don't."

Her smile dropped.

"Aw, Cammy, c'mon. You and I both know that if the Mud Boss hadn't broken an axle, you wouldn't have beaten me."

Camara frowned.

"So why don't you stop playing trucks with us big boys and go home and play with your dolls?"

Her old defense mechanism kicked in, and his twinkling eyes did nothing to soothe the anger rising in her. She spun the bill of her cap around, closed her eyes, and started counting. *One, two, three, four, five . . .*

Her eyes darted open. Even though he was teasing, Camara couldn't take it anymore. If looks could burn, he'd be a crispy critter with the fiery flames she shot his way. "Let me tell you something, mister. I didn't graduate at the top of my class from the best auto mechanic college in the world to play with dolls. I plan to keep on racing and to keep on winning. And there is nothing that you or any other chauvinistic male will say or do to stop me." Camara crossed her arms and glared at him, challenging him to refute her claim. She hated that she'd allowed him to rile her again. Attacking him made her feel about as slimy as the mud dripping from her body.

Chase took a step forward and flicked a piece of mud off her shoulder.

"What are you doing?"

"Knocking that chip off your shoulder."

One, two . . . So much for feeling slimy.

"Listen, bucko, the only chip on my shoulder is the one you put there with all your hateful, mean-spirited remarks and your constant put-downs. I've worked hard to get where I am. Y'all are just jealous because I can build and drive a truck as good as any man. I've proved it, too." She looked toward The Black Beast and then back at him. "I paid a hundred dollars at the junkyard for a rusted-out bucket of bolts and turned it into a clean, mean running machine. But no matter what I do or how hard I try, because I happen to be the wrong gender, y'all constantly put me and my truck down."

His macho, cool-as-chilled-watermelon expression melted.

"Well, just wait and see. My new modifications will speak for me." She twisted the bill on her cap forward. Not giving him a chance to retort, she whirled around. "See ya at the pits." She strutted toward her mud bog truck.

"Lord, that woman drives me crazy," Chase muttered. "I know I deserved what I got. I'm the one who started it. Why can't she see I was just having fun?"

In spite of her getting his goat, he chuckled. He had to admit just how fun it was watching her get all fired up. It tickled him that every time she got angry, she'd spin her cap around backward and close her eyes.

26

Those big brown eyes of hers, framed with thick eyelashes, glowed every time she talked about trucks and racing. She was as passionate about them as he was. His attraction for her had grown, along with his respect. "Lord, Ya gotta help me not to antagonize her anymore. Please."

He remembered her words about being cruel and felt instant remorse. She might appear tough on the outside, but he saw the hurt in her eyes when she mentioned how they'd all put her down. Even though he was just teasing her now, before he became a Christian he'd been as mean as a rabid dog, constantly putting her and her truck down — a fact he was now ashamed of. From now on, he'd watch his teasing of her. Plus, he needed to ask her to forgive him for being such a jerk.

First, Chase needed to get out of his muddy clothes. He looked over where Camara's truck and trailer were. Erik was using their water tank to hose the mud off her. Good thing he wasn't using the power sprayer. As tiny as she was, the pressure would send her flying. An idea struck him. He grabbed a towel and headed toward them.

"I'm next," Chase said, grinning.

Erik glanced at Chase and back at Camara. A smile of understanding spread across Erik's face. "So, y'all couldn't wait for the race, huh? Next time don't forget to take your trucks."

"Very funny, Erik. Ha, ha. Someday remind me to laugh." Camara narrowed her gaze at him menacingly.

Erik turned off the nozzle at the base of the tank and shook Chase's hand. "Good to see you again." He eyed Chase up and down. "From the looks of things, I'd say she bested ya."

Chase glanced at Camara, who quickly looked away. She snatched up a large towel and headed toward her Hummer.

"I have to admit, she did."

"Toss your towel over there." Erik jerked his head once toward the trailer. "I'll hose ya down."

While Erik sprayed him off, Chase watched Camara storm toward the bathroom.

She was an enigma for sure. Feminine and sweet. Rustic and gutsy. And feisty as all get-out when someone teased her about being a female mechanic — or about her Chevy losing — or about her short stature. That's when the feminine side of her evaporated like water drops on hot asphalt. Make no mistake about it, Camara Cole could

28

hold her own against any man in any race — including him. Many times she'd given him a run for his money. And anytime he had beaten her, it had been by a mere one-hundredth of a second.

Camara was one of Alabama's best mechanics. She knew her stuff, and Chase knew she could teach him a thing or two about building and repairing engines. He just wasn't ready to admit that to her or anyone else yet. He chuckled.

"What's so funny?" Erik asked.

"I was just thinking about your sister."

"Oh yeah?" Erik's eyebrows waggled.

"Not like that." Chase rolled his eyes. "I was just thinking that she's not afraid of a little mud or grease. And she sure doesn't back down from a challenge."

"That's for sure."

Both had a hearty laugh.

Then Chase remembered her comment about her modifications. Just what *did* she have under that hood? He'd soon find out. And he could hardly wait.

CHAPTER 2

Fed up with Chase's constant Chevy-bashing, short jokes, blond jokes, and female-mechanic slamming, Camara stormed off. Even though he was only teasing, she had heard enough to last her a lifetime. "You just wait and see, Chase," she grumbled under her breath. "My Chevy's gonna surprise you today." She grabbed a set of extra clothes from her Hummer and headed toward the women's restroom. Her body shook from the cold hosing down.

Inside the bathroom stall, Camara changed quickly. While tucking in her yellow T-shirt, she noticed her grease-stained nails and sighed at the futility of making them look nice. By the time she finished checking things under the hood today, they'd look a whole lot worse than they did now. She had to make sure everything ran in tip-top shape.

Usually Swamper Speedway only held mud bog races twice a month. But because mud slinging had become so popular, the owner decided to make it a weekly event. He had announced that the winner of this season's mud bog racing would receive the honor of having a replica of their bogging vehicle, along with its name, sported on all of next year's trophies, so it was even more important to win this year.

Not only would she be the first female to win, but she would finally prove that she could build and drive a truck as good as any man. Maybe then the harassment would stop.

She stuffed her clothes in her bag and smiled. After losing precious seconds at the start-up line, she had finally figured out how to gain a second or two — a stall converter. Today she'd see if her efforts paid off. She could ramp up the rpms until the torque converter engaged and then her truck wouldn't stall anymore.

It was the best four hundred dollars she'd ever spent. And if that didn't work, she knew what she'd found in a popular off-road magazine would.

She put on her jean jacket and hugged it tight, relishing its warmth. If Chase hadn't thrown her into the mud pit, she wouldn't be this cold. What had come over him anyway?

He sure had been acting different lately. She wasn't at all sure she liked the new Chase. At least with the old one, she knew how to act around him: barb for barb, jab for jab. When he'd slam her Chevy, she'd slam his Ford. Truth be known, she loved his '34 Ford Coupe. Camara pictured how macho and handsome Chase looked sitting in it.

Her thoughts drifted to earlier. She couldn't believe Chase had almost kissed her. She wiped her lips off with her shirtsleeve and scrunched her face. She would have decked him if he had.

Camara gathered the rest of her things and stuffed them in her duffel bag. After dropping it at her Hummer, she headed toward the entry booth.

"Good morning, Sam."

"Morning." Sam's bronzed tan made his bright smile appear even whiter, and his white hair made him look much older than forty-three. Camara smiled at his familiar face. If Sam wasn't making sure the contestants completed their entry forms, signed their insurance waivers, paid their entry moneys, and received their contestant numbers, he was out flagging or doing any other volunteer job that needed doing.

She took the proffered clipboard with the attached entry form and a rules pamphlet. Holding up the pamphlet, she sent Sam a questioning look.

"Something new this year," Sam replied to her unspoken question. "You might want to go over it before you enter, Camara."

Camara walked over to a picnic bench and sat down. Tapping the pen against her lips, she pondered whether she should mention the changes she'd made to her bog truck. Places she usually raced had Modified, Super Modified, Stock, and Super Stock classes, but because Swamper Speedway only ran an 8-cylinder Open class where anything was permissible and tire size didn't matter, she decided against mentioning the nitrous oxide system.

Finished filling out the form, Camara handed her entry fee and form to Sam. "Thanks, Sam."

"Good luck today, Camara."

Camara removed her favorite yellow Chevy emblem cap, tossed it on the front seat of her Hummer, and sprinted over to The Black Beast. Once inside her 1974 Chevy bog truck, she fastened her harness and watched as Erik moved her step stool out of the way.

Giving her a thumbs-up sign, he said, "Go show 'em how it's done, girl."

Thankful that her brother believed in her and had always been there for her, Camara smiled.

Admiration for her six-foot-tall, athletically built brother made her sigh. Being the youngest and only girl in her family, Camara had always followed in her closest sibling's footsteps. Everything Erik did, she did — including building and racing mud bog trucks. In fact, Erik had raced boggers for years until he decided driving a monster truck sounded more interesting. Perhaps someday she'd build and race a monster truck, too.

Looking at the instrument panel, she flipped two toggle switches and simultaneously pressed the starter button and racing gas pedal. The engine roared to life. Shivers of delight raced up and down Camara's spine. Strapping on her helmet, she put the truck in gear and drove toward the mud pits.

Chase pulled up to the pit next to her. She smiled. *Good.*

Even though it was a timed event, her wish of running side by side with him came true. Excitement bubbled inside her, knowing the men who belittled her would be watching as she blew off Chase's doors.

Pride goes before a fall. Guilt tugged at her soul, but the desire to prove to everyone that she was a proficient competitor drove her harder. A hint of sadness dabbled over Camara. If only they would accept her.

Over the PA system, a voice announced: "Lining up at pit number one is contestant number 23, Chase Lamar, driving the Mud Boss, a 1934 Ford Coupe with 39.5 boggers. Powered with a 351 Cleveland small block."

Camara watched as they hooked up the pull cable to Chase's receiver hitch. Her gaze followed the other end of the cable where a backhoe sat ready to pull them out if need be. Without it, if any of them got stuck in the middle of the mud pit, they'd have no way of getting out. Camara was grateful to whoever thought up the idea. She might like mud racing, but she didn't want to get out in the middle of the pit.

She watched the flagman motion Chase forward. When he reached the start-up line, the flagger jerked his fist shut. Chase stopped and revved his engine. Expectant faces peered out from behind the protective chain-link fence. Men, women, and children of all ages clapped when Chase's name was announced.

She hoped they would be as excited to see her as they were to see Chase.

"At pit number two, we have contestant number 24, Camara Cole, driving a 1974 modified Chevy pickup, The Black Beast. Camara's running 38-inch Super Swamper TSL tires with a 400 small block engine."

Camara glanced at the crowd and grinned. More than half the crowd stood clapping.

"C'mon, Cammy! You can do it!" she heard Erik yelling above the noise. She glanced toward the nearby contestant's pit. Erik stood at the end of the orange fence blockade along with her dad, mom, and brothers Tony and Slick. All of them gave her a thumbs-up. *Thank You, Lord, for a family who supports me.* She looked to see if anyone was there for Chase. The only person she noticed was his friend John.

Turning her attention back to the task at hand, she quickly perused the deep ruts made by the other drivers. At the end of the mud pit was a thick muddy wall that the other drivers hadn't penetrated. It seemed to mock her. Strong determination rose up inside her. She'd show that mud pit she could break its barrier.

She studied the ruts. If she went to the left of the deepest one, she'd end up out of

control and perhaps over the side, disquali-
fying herself. She looked toward the right.
Noting a fresh spot where no one had gone,
she decided to try it.

That wall would not best her. She'd show
it who was boss.

The flagman motioned Camara forward.
She inched her way until he signaled her to
stop.

Goose bumps rose on Camara's flesh. Her
adrenaline kicked into overdrive. She tugged
on her leather gloves and clutched the steering wheel. Her right leg started shaking.

Chase revved his engine again.

Not about to be outdone, Camara pressed
the pedal to the floor. *Rrrruuun rrrruuun.* She
let up, allowing the engine to idle. *Crr crr crr
crr.*

She pressed it again.

Over the loud rumbling inside the cab of
her truck, she heard the crowd roaring.

Chase tapped his pedal fast two times. She
looked over at him. He waved a pointed
finger, smiled, and gave her a thumbs-up.

What's that all about? Humpft. She liked it
better when he was an arrogant jerk.

The flagman raised the green flag.

Camara flipped the master switch. Every
nerve stood on end. She fidgeted against
the harness.

With her left foot on the brake, Camara pressed the gas, ramping up the rpms.

The flag dropped.

She slipped her left foot off the brake and floored the gas pedal. The Black Beast lurched forward then dropped into the pit, dipping her stomach right along with it.

The front tires pulled to the right. Arms tensed, she clutched the steering wheel tighter. With all her might, Camara jerked the wheel left. The rear stayed to the right, and she had to correct back to the right.

Her tires gripped their way through the deep mud, slinging the muck a good twenty-five feet into the air and onto her windshield.

Using all her bodybuilding strength, she tightened her grip to keep The Black Beast headed down the center of the pit. She darted a quick side glance toward Chase but couldn't see him because of all the mud flying.

Nearing the end of the pit and that mocking mud wall, she mashed the secret weapon button on the steering wheel with her thumb. Surging with power, The Black Beast shot forward. Quickly, she broke through the mud wall, raised her thumb, and up and out of the pit she flew.

Realizing she beat Chase, she pumped her

fist and whooped and hollered, "Yes! Yes! Yes!"

She stuck her head out the window so she could see where she was going as she drove to the contestant's pit and revved the engine before shutting it off. She jerked her helmet off and shook her hair loose.

Erik slung the door open, yanked her out of her truck, and swung her around. "Way to go, Cam!"

When he put her down, she held her breath, waiting to hear her and Chase's times.

"Well, folks, each contestant runs twice, and we combine their total times. For this run, Camara's time is 9.26, and Chase Lamar's time is 11.83. . . ." The announcer's voice faded as several people came up to congratulate Camara on a great run. She thanked them, keeping her eye out for Chase. Her heart did a funny flip-flop when she saw him heading toward her.

"Congratulations, Camara. Nice run." Chase grabbed her hand and shook it, holding it longer than necessary. Vibration ran up her arm from his touch. Uncomfortable, she snatched it back. What was wrong with her? That had never happened before.

She blew away the unwanted feelings.

"Thanks," she said. Then she turned

around and talked to Lolly.

Chase stepped back. Whatever she had under that hood had worked. He walked back to his Coupe and started hosing it down. When he saw his father heading toward him with a scowl on his face, Chase cringed.

"What are you doing letting that Cole woman beat you?" his father spit out.

"Hi, Dad."

"No son of mine is going to let a girl, let alone one of them Coles, get the best of him. What happened out there?"

"I didn't let her win, if that's what you're thinking. She beat me fair and square." Chase chuckled. "Whatever modifications she did to her truck worked." As soon as his gaze met his dad's disapproving glare, Chase's smile faded.

"Well, we'll just have to find out now, won't we? You took care of it in the past; you can do it again."

That was in the past, Chase wanted to tell him. But as angry as his dad was right now, Chase knew better than to say anything.

At one time, Chase had wanted to make Camara look bad, too. More to please his father than anything. But secretly he was jealous of her. She could outbuild and out-

40

drive most men, and she was an amazing mechanic. He'd heard her praised by lots of people. However, since accepting Christ as his Savior, he no longer cared about showing her up. Mud slinging was a sport he loved and nothing else. Well, almost. Sure, he wanted to win. What man wouldn't? It was tough losing to anyone, much less a woman.

"Chase, did you hear me?" His father's raucous voice broke through his musings.

Chase hated how his dad could make him feel five years old again.

"What are you going to do about it?" The hatred in his eyes made Chase's skin crawl.

Even though he knew why his dad was so bitter toward the Coles, he no longer wanted to take on his dad's offense as his own. Sure, at one time he had. Especially after Camara had become his biggest competitor. Rather than face his dad's displeasure at a Cole beating him, Chase had started messing with her bog truck. At first it was exciting, thinking of different ways to make The Black Beast run badly. Each time he'd beat Camara's time, his dad had praised him. Approval from his dad was something Chase sought. But after giving his life to Christ, his desire switched from wanting to please his earthly father to wanting to please his heavenly Father. And the difference was huge.

Chase drew in a deep breath. It was time he started standing up to his father. And there was no time like the present.

"Not a thing, Dad." Chase refused to flinch under his dad's evil stare.

"Well, somebody should." His father stormed off.

Something about the way his dad said it caused a deep, sinking feeling in the pit of his stomach. Hard telling what his father was capable of these days. Whatever it was, Chase knew it was bound to be bad. He shuddered. From now on, Chase would have to keep an eye on his dad — especially around Camara.

CHAPTER 3

Camara and Chase had just made their final run of the day. She pulled next to her trailer, shut off The Black Beast, and held her breath waiting for her final time. She glanced at the dashboard and flipped off the master switch and all her toggle switches.

Hickory smoke from a nearby barbecue wafted up her nose, making her stomach growl. She patted her abdomen. Until she heard her time, her empty belly would have to wait.

"Are you ready for this, folks?" The announcer's voice echoed through the loudspeaker. "We have a new record here at Swamper Speedway. Camara Cole's time is . . ." He paused.

Camara's heart froze. "C'mon."

"8.78! Congratulations, Camara." The announcer's voice faded as she slung open the truck door and jumped out.

Her dad, mom, and three brothers gathered around her, hugging and congratulating her.

"I'm proud of you, baby girl," Daddy whispered in her ear. Her family stepped back, making room for other well-wishers.

"It's my turn," Lolly singsonged. She spun Camara around and gave her a big hug. "I wish it were Stan breaking the speedway's record, but . . ." She looked around. "If it had to be someone else, I'm so glad it was you. All those men will be eating barbecued crow tonight, won't they?" Lolly hugged Camara again. "Oh, here comes Chase. I'll talk to you later." With that, Lolly darted off.

Camara turned just as Chase neared her.

"Congratulati—"

"Told ya I'd blow your doors off today," Camara cut Chase off and sent him a playful but prideful grin. "Now what was that you said again about beating me?" She placed her finger on her lips and squinted. "Better get rid of that hunk-o-junk Ford and invest in a Chevy," she teased. "I know where there's a great Chevrolet dealership who'd give ya an awesome deal."

Chase shook his head, sighing. "When are you gonna grow up, Cammy? It's not about winning but about how you play the game."

Her eyes widened then narrowed as the

memory of catching him under the hood of The Black Beast the previous year streaked through her mind. "The only thing *you* know about playing the game is messing with my bog truck and playing mind games before a race. Well, it didn't work today, did it?" She smiled again smugly, grateful she had shown up him and all the other guys.

Taking a step backward, Chase gazed at her. "Look, I know I've tinkered with your truck before and that I tried to psych you out before a race. I also know I've played a big part in you being defensive." He glanced at the ground then back at her. "I'm sorry. For all of it."

Stunned by his humility, her mouth fell open and her pride siphoned from her, leaving her feeling foolish.

Chase tilted his head sideways and sniffed the air. "Nitrous. You're running NOS? So that's your power booster."

Camara flipped her eyebrows upward. "Among other things." She smirked, feeling arrogant and rather pleased with herself.

Chase shook his head. He glanced at her truck. "Hope that pride of yours doesn't destroy you. Enjoy your victory, Camara."

He turned and strode off, stopping at the announcer's stand briefly before heading toward his bogger. Pride deflated from Camara. Chase's words stung. Hadn't her father said over and over again that her pride would be the ruin of her and true winners never boast? Her victory lost its sweetness. She'd been so busy worrying about winning and proving to the guys that she was just as good as them that she forgot all about building inner character and walking in love.

Staring at the ground, she scuffed her toe in the dirt as she thought about how she and Chase had constantly teased and bantered back and forth over the years about winning and who would beat whom. But this time, she'd gone too far. She could kick herself. Would she ever learn to shut her mouth and feel confident enough in her own abilities without trying to prove herself all the time?

Chase felt sorry for Camara. Didn't she know what a desirable woman she was until she opened her mouth? All that boasting turned his stomach, but unfortunately not his heart. His heart had changed toward her when he saw how she treated other people at church. She always made it a point to talk to the elderly and offered to help them. Whenever there was something going on to help another in need, Camara was first in

46

line to volunteer. Oftentimes he wondered how she found time to work at her dad's dealership all day, keep her bogger in top running condition, and help those in need. He guessed she'd always been that way, but he was so busy trying to please his dad and trying to oust her that he'd never taken the time to see the goodness in her, nor did he care to at the time. But now he wanted to know her better.

Chase grabbed the sprayer and turned on the generator. Bent at the waist, he sprayed under the fender wells, tossing an idea back and forth in his mind. Maybe he would let Camara win this year. After all, he couldn't care less about winning anymore. His dad was the one who pushed him to succeed, saying it would be great advertising for his companies.

Realization hit him like a Mack truck. Chase straightened. Like everyone else in his dad's life, Chase had been a pawn to further his father's empire.

His dad never cared about him. His only concern was Chase's winning because it benefited him.

He remembered when his father had discovered his only son had "gotten religion."

"Someday you'll take over for me, son."

Arrogance oozed from his voice. "But to succeed, you'll have to get rid of that religious nonsense. All of them Christians are brainwashed, poor folks. What's really important in this life is money and power. And I've got both."

Thanks to the millions Granddad had left him.

Chase wished he could get his dad to understand that money wasn't the answer. And what Chase had found wasn't religion — it was relationship. His relationship with the Lord was his number-one priority now.

"Will Camara Cole, Chase Lamar, Bobby-Rae Wallers, and Trey Daum come to the announcer's stand, please?"

The announcer's voice broke through Chase's reverie. He turned to his friend John. "Hey, buddy, will ya finish washing the mud off my Coupe for me?"

"Sure. No problem."

Chase handed the sprayer to John and walked away. "I owe ya one."

"You owe me two now," John hollered at him, chuckling.

He sure did owe John. He was the one who never gave up inviting him to church. He chuckled as he thought about how they'd met. Chase had just finished running and was heading toward the contestant's pit. His windshield was covered with mud, so he had hung his head out the window to see where he was going. He was concentrating so hard watching his side that he failed to watch the other side. When he heard a thump, he slammed on his brake and jumped out. John, a muscle-bound, hulking African-American man the size of a sycamore tree, lay on the ground in front of his Coupe.

"I'm sorry, man, I didn't see you. Are you okay?"

"I'm fine." John had started to rise. Chase reached out his hand to help him up. As John rose, Chase slowly leaned his head back, looking up at him. He guessed John weighed in around 240 pounds, mostly muscle, and was about six-foot-five. He normally would have found someone that tall intimidating, but the kindness in John's eyes and his large smile put him at ease. "I should have been watching where I was going. I know y'all can't see where you're going after running. It was my fault."

Chase had been so stunned that John didn't cuss or yell or anything. With all of his family's money, most people looked for an excuse to sue them. Not this guy. He took the blame. That was the beginning of their friendship.

Thank You, Lord, for John. He smiled as he approached the announcer's booth and stood next to Camara.

"Camara," Dan, the owner of Swamper Speedway, said. "It's come to our attention that you ran nitrous in your truck."

"Yes, sir." She shot a dirty look Chase's way and focused her attention back on Dan.

"Do you have a fire extinguisher in your bog truck?"

"No, sir." She frowned. "Why?"

"Did you read the pamphlet Sam handed out to every driver?"

Camara turned pale and shook her head.

"It states in there that anyone running nitrous oxide is required to have a fire extinguisher. And that anyone caught without one would not be allowed to race. Had we known about the NOS before you ran, we wouldn't have let you. I'm sorry, Camara. Because you didn't have an extinguisher, we have to disqualify you from the race today, and your time will be stripped from the records. First place will now go to Chase. Second to Trey, and third to Bobby-Rae."

Camara stepped back as if in shock. She blinked several times as she darted glances at the other male contestants. "But . . . but you can't . . . I didn't know. I worked so hard. I . . ." Her blinking increased. She turned her face away from their view.

Chase scanned the men's faces, trying to see them from her point of view. What he saw made his heart wrench. Poor Camara. Judging by the smirks on several of their faces, he got a glimpse of what she'd been up against, and what he, too, had put her through.

When he looked back at her, she whirled and ran, but not before he noticed a tear slide down her cheek. Chase's heart broke for her. Erik had mentioned to him that Camara hated for anyone to see her cry because she wanted to fit in and be one of the guys. One of these days he would get her to see that it was okay to let people see her vulnerable side. Then maybe she wouldn't run off. But who knew. Some habits are hard to break.

He looked at Dan. "I don't mind, Dan, if you let Camara have my points and trophy. She didn't know the new rules."

"Chase, I know you're trying to do what you think is right here, but just because she didn't read the pamphlet doesn't mean she can get away with breaking the rules. I would have had to do the same thing no matter who it was. Trust me. I hate having to do this. Camara deserved it. She flew through that pit."

Camara's shocked, hurt-filled face raced through Chase's mind. She'd obviously worked hard setting her truck up to run nitrous. She had outraced them all. He couldn't stand it that he was the one to take the trophy from her. It meant everything to her and nothing to him.

He had to find her and see if there was something he could say or do to comfort her. "Congratulations, y'all," he said, shaking Bobby-Rae's and Trey's hands. He hurried to find Camara. But the only thing he saw was Camara leaving in her Hummer, pulling The Black Beast behind.

For the twentieth time, Camara reprimanded herself. She had a feeling she should have mentioned the nitrous. But no, pride wouldn't let her. She didn't want anyone to know. She just wanted to show all of them she could do it. Well, she did it all right. She blew it big time. Camara slammed her hand on the steering wheel. "I knew I should have read that stupid pamphlet."

With darkness settling over the long stretch of empty road, the abandoned cotton fields with some of the old cotton still clinging to them held a certain eeriness.

Normally she loved this area. Because it hadn't been farmed in years, nobody ever came out this way, so it was her escape from the hubbub of the city and a place to be alone when the pressure of having to prove herself became too much. But with darkness falling fast, the shadows from the massive oak trees loomed like big monsters reaching their strangling arms toward her.

Never in her life had she felt more humiliated than she did now. Tears blurred her eyes. Camara struggled to see the road. She leaned toward the glove compartment and popped it open. Glancing back at the road and then back again at the box of Kleenex, she tugged a couple out. When she looked back at the road, her eyes widened and she jerked the steering wheel, fighting to avoid hitting a deer.

The deer survived; however, her Hummer rammed head-long into a deep ditch, bashing Camara's head against the steering wheel then whipping her backward. Spots twinkled before her eyes. Camara struggled to stay conscious, but everything turned dark.

Camara squinted as she opened her eyes. The interior of her vehicle was pitch-black. Her head throbbed. She placed her hand on the back of her neck and rolled it slowly. It hurt to move.

How long had she been here? She pushed the clock button on the dash. 9:58 p.m. Peering up at the sky, she focused on the Big Dipper, and it all came back to her. She was out near the abandoned fields. Groaning, she laid her head back against the headrest for a moment and then leaned forward.

A chorus of howling coyotes caused the hair on the back of her neck to rise. Were they nearby? She shuddered.

Her hands shook as she put the Hummer in reverse and pressed the gas. It didn't move an inch. She put it in drive and hit the gas. Nothing but spinning tires. Knowing the trailer must be jackknifed, Camara flipped the overhead light on, opened the center console, and groaned. Once more, she'd forgotten to grab her cell phone.

Her head started reeling, and she felt nauseous. "Lord, please send someone to help me." She laid her head back against the headrest and closed her heavy eyelids.

She awoke to the sound of a vehicle. Even in the midst of her grogginess, she recognized that sound. "Oh no, not him. Lord, please don't let it be him."

The door on her Hummer opened.

"Cammy, thank God I found you."

Camara groaned. *Is this some kind of joke, Lord? You sent the enemy to help me?*

CHAPTER 4

What Chase saw when he opened the door to Camara's Hummer turned his stomach. Her cheek and neck were caked with dried blood from the nasty gash on her forehead.

"Are you hurt anywhere?" Chase fought to keep his voice steady as he drew near and scanned her body. "Besides your head."

"What are you doing here?" she asked then winced.

"I was worried about you."

She raised her brows and shivered. Chase removed his light jacket and draped it over her shoulders.

"I called your house. When I kept getting your answering machine, I finally called Erik. He said not to worry about you. But every time I prayed for you, I couldn't shake the feeling something was wrong." Chase removed his cap and ran his hand over his spiked hair. "Every time I asked God if He wanted me to do something, I felt like I should go look for you. So I did." He shrugged. "That was hours ago. I almost gave up until I spotted your rig."

Her face softened then quickly turned into a frown. "Why were you trying to call me?"

"It's a long story. I'll explain it on the way to the hospital."

Before he had a chance to help her out, she swung her legs around and hopped down. His jacket fell from her shoulders as she slumped to the ground. Chase grabbed her arms and eased her up. "You okay?"

Camara closed her eyes and opened them slowly. "I twisted my ankle," she whimpered, "and my head is spinning."

Not asking her permission, he scooped her into his arms and carried her up the steep embankment toward his pickup. When she didn't argue, his concern grew.

The driver's side door stood open. Balancing Camara, Chase stepped on the side-board and gently sat her in the middle of the seat. Making sure she was secure, he ran back to her Hummer, snatched up his coat, and slipped and slid his way up the steep ditch. He hopped in his truck and shut the door.

"Wait!" Camara clutched his arm. "I can't leave my Hummer and bog truck out here."

Chase flipped the interior light on. "Look,

Cam, I'm not worried about that right now. I need to get ya to the hospital. That gouge in your head is pretty deep." He engaged the clutch and put it in first gear. "I'll call someone to take care of them."

"No!" Camara's voice filled with desperation.

He stopped the truck and faced her.

"Please?" The pleading look in her eyes unsettled Chase. He struggled with the need to get her to the hospital and the desire to succumb to Camara's plea to take care of her vehicles first.

Camara glanced at his belt where his cell phone was clasped. "May I use your phone to call Erik? He can get the shop's tow truck and haul them for me."

Knowing how much she prized The Black Beast, Chase relented. Nodding, he unclipped his cell phone and handed it to her. He put the truck in neutral and set the emergency brake.

Glancing over, he watched Camara punch in some numbers then put the phone to her ear. Each movement looked as if it pained her to make it.

"No, it's me, Camara. I'm using Chase's cell phone." She sighed heavily. "Yes, Chase's phone. Erik," her voice sounded strained and annoyed, "forget that for now.

58

I need a favor. Could you and Tony grab Daddy's tow truck and come out to the abandoned fields and —" She closed her eyes. Frustration etched her forehead. "I know I shouldn't have come out here, but I did. Please, Erik." Her voice softened, breaking Chase's heart. She looked so vulnerable.

"I know it's late, but will you *please* come and get my vehicles? I don't wanna leave them here." She paused. Chase felt funny eavesdropping, but where was he supposed to go? He tried focusing on the chirping katydids outside and the million stars filling the inky night, but his ears kept tuning to Camara's voice.

"No, I swerved to miss a deer, and it high-centered in a ditch." She pulled the phone away. "Erik, please don't yell. I have a splitting headache." Tears slipped down her cheeks.

Chase wanted to pull her into his arms and comfort her, but he knew better.

"Yes, I'm fine." Her voice quavered. "Please, will ya take care of them?" More tears. "Thank you, Erik. I'm really sorry to bother you." She slowly nodded. "Okay. Just a minute." She handed the phone to Chase. "Erik wants to talk to you." She faced forward and stared out his windshield.

"Hey."

"Is Camara really okay?" The concern in Erik's voice for his little sister touched Chase. The only people who cared about him like that were his twenty-year-old sister, Heather, and his mother. But they had moved closer to Heather's college about a hundred miles from Chase's house. He sighed inwardly. If only his dad hadn't forced Heather and his mom to give up Christ or get out, they would still be living at his dad's house and he'd get to spend time with them. Chase often thanked God he had his own place, or his father would have booted him out, too, when he chose to follow Christ.

"Chase." The panic in Erik's voice snapped Chase from his musings.

"Sorry. She has a nasty cut on her forehead and a twisted ankle, but other than that, she seems okay." He glanced at Camara, who wiped her eyes and rubbed her nose. Again he fought the urge to console her, but not knowing how she would react, he thought it best if he didn't.

"Are you going to take her to the hospital?"

"Yeah."

"Then tell her I'll call Mom and Dad, and I'll be there as soon as I get The Black Beast for her." There was a short pause. "That truck means everything to her."

"Don't I know it." Chase heaved a dry chuckle.

"Let me know as soon as you find out anything."

"Will do. Talk to ya later." He flipped his phone off and attached it to his belt.

He looked over at Camara and was about to let her know what Erik said, but he stopped. Her chin touched her chest, and her shoulders shook. When he heard her sob, Chase didn't care what she thought. He carefully pulled her into his arms. She made no attempt to push him away, so he rocked her soothingly.

"It's okay, Cammy. You don't have to be tough all the time, ya know."

Her only response was the shaking of her shoulders. When she stopped crying, she whispered against his shirt, "Were you try- ing to call me earlier so you could gloat because I blew it big time today?" Her timid voice held no bitterness, only a heartbreak- ing vulnerability.

"No. I called to see how you were. When you drove off like you did, I was worried about you." He gently grasped Camara's chin and turned her to face him. Torment and tears glimmered in her big brown eyes, crushing his heart. Trying to gain control of the fresh, unexplained emotions he was experiencing toward her, Chase cleared his throat. "I tried talking them into letting you keep the trophy. After all, you deserved it. But Dan said he couldn't."

She blinked, and her wide eyes stared at him. "Why would you do that?"

"Because you beat me, and I care — ," Chase caught himself. He didn't want her to know how much she affected him. "Look, I need to get you to the hospital." He pointed to her forehead. "That cut looks pretty nasty. How long have you been out here anyway?"

"Since about nine thirty."

Chase groaned. "That was . . ." He twisted his wrist and checked his watch: 12:47. "More than three hours ago."

His heart ached knowing she'd been stranded that long. Releasing her from his arms, he started to leave.

"Can't we wait till Erik gets here?"

"Look, no one's been by here in over three hours." He nodded toward her vehicles. "I think they'll be safe."

"Could you at least lock them up for me?" Chase knew what it cost her to ask him, her enemy, for help.

He sighed in surrender. "Does Erik have a

set of keys?"

"Yes."

He nodded and quickly took care of it. When he got back in the truck, he flipped the interior light off and headed toward Swamper City.

The pounding in Camara's head reminded her of an African ritual drumbeat. With each throb came sharp pain. She desperately wanted to rest her head and go to sleep, but first she needed to ask Chase something. She looked at him. "Chase?"

"Yeah." He glanced at her then back at the road.

Her gaze slipped to her fingers in the darkness. "After you smelled the NOS, I saw you stop by the announcer's stand. Are you the one who reported it?"

In the dark interior, Camara saw the white of Chase's wide eyes. "No, I didn't. I can understand how you might have thought it was me, especially considering what I've done to you in the past. But I stopped by the stand and told Dan that with the way you just ran I had my job cut out for me this summer." The lights on the dashboard cast shadows on his face when he glanced at her. "You did a great job with that truck." He turned his gaze back toward the road.

Camara's brows rose. She must have hit her head harder than she'd thought. Did Chase just say she'd done a great job on her truck?

"But," he said as he glanced at her with a teasing smile, "ya still need to get a Ford."

"Oh, you." She slapped him on the arm then instantly regretted the action. The quick movement caused searing pain. Camara clutched her head.

"What's wrong?"

"My head's killing me."

Chase accelerated the engine.

Camara opened her eyes. Her head rested against Chase's shoulder, and she was snuggled up against him as if . . . Camara tossed the unwelcome thought aside and quickly scooted over. The quick movement caused shooting pain through her ankle and head.

Embarrassed, she mumbled, "Sorry."

Chase glanced at her and back at the road. "For what?"

What could she say? *For resting my head on your shoulder and sitting so close to you that I was practically on your lap?* She glanced at the clock on his dash: 1:33. Instant remorse smacked her as she realized the hospital was at least another fifteen minutes away. *Poor Chase.* "For making you stay up so late."

He reached over, wrapped his hand around hers, and gazed at her. "You didn't make me do anything. I came of my own free will." He smiled and turned his attention toward the road. "I'm just glad I followed the Holy Spirit's leading and came looking for you. You might have been out there for days before anyone found you."

"Nah, my parents or Erik would have come looking for me eventually."

"I don't think so. When I called Erik, he told me not to worry about you because you do this a lot and you'd show up at work on Monday morning."

The enormity of Camara's situation bulldozed over her. She drew in a shaky breath. "You're right." She lowered her lids and spoke softly, "Thank you, Chase."

He reached over and squeezed her hand again. His calloused hand felt warm, and a strange tingling sensation powered up her arm even as he let go to put his hand back on the steering wheel.

"Thank the Lord, Cammy. He's the One who laid you on my heart." His tone had a strange huskiness to it.

It occurred to Camara that ever since Chase had accepted Jesus as his Savior, he'd actually become a nice guy. At singles night at church, he and Erik had become close friends. And Erik was a great judge of character. Maybe she should cut Chase some slack and give him the benefit of the doubt.

From the corner of her eye, she watched him. A sensation that could only be described as tickling feathers tingled her stomach.

To think she'd been frustrated at God for sending Chase. Now she didn't mind at all. In fact, she was almost grateful. Subconsciously she touched her forehead. She really must have hit her head harder than she'd thought. She was getting soft where Chase Lamar was concerned, and she wasn't sure that was such a safe thing to do.

CHAPTER 5

Camara gazed out her kitchen window and watched the sun rise. Taking the last bite of her grits, she marveled at how the raindrops slid off the yellow bell bushes and yet remained stationary on the red daylilies, purple impatiens, pink and white lantanas, and black-eyed Susans. The beautiful blooming flowers, along with the hot pink blooms on the crepe myrtle trees, brightened Camara's yard and her gloomy mood. After being stuck inside for six days, she couldn't wait to get out of the house. "Erik, where are you?"

The doorbell rang.

She tucked her crutches under her arms and hobbled into the living room.

Erik popped his head inside. "Hey, Cam. Ya ready?"

"Sure am, bubba. Just waiting for you."

"You need help with anything?"

"Just my backpack." She pointed toward

the floor.

Erik opened her door, and Camara stepped out. Dampness, mingled with honeysuckle and fresh-cut grass, wafted up her nose.

The sight of The Black Beast caused a thrill to race up her spine. One thing was for certain: She was a mud-boggin' fanatic. As she hobbled her way across the wet grass, moisture from last night's rain clung to the toe of the tennis shoe on her good foot, soaking it. She stopped for a moment and allowed the sun's morning rays to penetrate her pores, warming her through.

"Come on, Cam."

"Spoilsport. Give me a break. I've been indoors all week. I forgot how nice the sun feels."

"You sure you're up for this?" His brown eyes held concern.

"I'm fine." She hobbled to her Hummer. "It was a minor concussion, that's all."

Erik laid her crutches against her vehicle and lifted her up as if she weighed no more than a hummingbird. Making sure she was situated, he placed the crutches alongside her and closed the door.

Erik hopped in the driver's side and slid the key in the ignition.

"Now don't forget to . . ."

Erik pointed a stern finger at her. "Cammy." The impatience in his voice was evident. "I know what you're fixin' to say."

"Sorry. It just seems so strange having someone else driving my vehicle. It'll be even weirder watching you run The Black Beast today." She shifted her weight toward Erik. "You brought a fire extinguisher, right?"

"For the fiftieth time, yes."

"Whatever you do," she said, pointing her finger at him, "don't forget to make sure the nitrous switch is off and that the hose isn't kinked before you fire the Beast up. And when you go to take off into the pit —"

"Camara! You act like I've never driven your truck before, or any other truck for that matter."

"Sorry. It's just that you've never run NOS before, and I didn't want you to forget."

"How could I? We've been over this a million times already." At his frustrated look, Camara knew she'd gone too far.

"Sorry. I'm just nervous." She giggled. "I have drilled you all week, haven't I?"

"Nah." Erik started the Hummer, looked over his shoulder, and steered the vehicle onto the road. "Only six days." He sent her

69

a teasing smile. "You're one day shy of a week."

What would she do without Erik? He was the best brother a girl could have. "Erik."

"Yeah." He glanced at her then back at the road.

"Thanks."

"For what?"

"For being you. And for always being there for me."

He leaned over and ruffled her hair. "That's what big brothers are for. Besides, someone has to keep ya out of trouble."

"That's for sure." They both laughed.

Chase removed the nylon straps from the Mud Boss even as he watched for Camara's vehicle to pull in. She probably wondered why he hadn't called her. There was no way he could explain to her why he hadn't. When his dad found out he'd helped Camara, he came unglued.

"If I ever hear you talking to that . . . that Cole girl again, I'll disown you," his dad sneered.

"Dad. That's ridiculous. I see her every weekend at the mud bogs. I can't just ignore her."

"You can, and you will."

Knowing it was a no-win situation, Chase

decided rather than argue with his dad he would instead make an appointment with Pastor Stephans to find out just how far a person was supposed to go in honoring their parents. Were children supposed to do whatever their parents said, even if they were twenty-three years old and living on their own? Chase loved the Lord and wanted to obey Him, but his dad's obsessive hatred toward the Cole family was driving Chase crazy.

Jumping inside the Mud Boss, Chase backed it off the trailer and pulled alongside his Ford pickup. After revving the engine a couple of times, he shut it off. He caught sight of Camara's yellow Hummer. His heart switched to high gear. Not sure what to do, he sat and watched.

Camara scanned the contestants' pit looking for Chase. She thought surely he would have called or dropped by this past week to see how she was doing, but he hadn't. Not that she wanted him to, but after his attentiveness toward her, she thought he might. Spotting his rig, her pulse shifted into overdrive.

Erik opened her door and helped her gain her footing on the uneven ground. Camara gimped back to her trailer and tried manipulating her crutches around so she could unlatch one of the straps attached to The Black Beast.

"Camara Chevelle Cole! What do you think you're doing?" Erik picked her up and moved her aside. "You're gonna hurt yourself. I'll take care of this." He unclamped one of the straps. "Why don't ya go enter me?" His frustrated look said he wasn't in the mood to brook any argument from her.

"Fine. I was only trying to help."

"Listen, sis. I've got it handled, okay?" He grasped her upper arms and looked her square in the eye. "Trust me."

"Thanks, bubba." She gripped her crutches and made her way toward the entry booth.

Between the high humidity and the exertion of using crutches on the loose gravel, Camara was panting by the time she reached the booth.

"Good morning," Camara greeted Sam's back.

He turned, and his eyes widened. "What happened to you?"

"I tore the ligaments in my foot." She hoped he wouldn't probe further.

"How'd you get that nasty cut?" He leaned forward and studied it.

Too embarrassed to tell him, Camara

changed the subject. "Listen, Sam. I won't be driving my truck today. Erik will."

Sam nodded and handed her the forms. Camara took a quick look behind her. "Do you mind if I stand here and fill this out? I promise if someone comes I'll move out of the way."

"No problem."

Camara hustled to fill out the form.

"Did you bring a fire extinguisher today?" Sam asked.

Camara looked up from the form. The hopeful look in his eyes made her smile. "Oh yeah," she said, drawing out the words.

She reached in the back pocket of her jeans and pulled out the ready-made check and handed it, along with the entry form, to Sam. Without looking, Camara swung her crutches around and smacked into something, throwing her off balance. Her hair flew across her face. Someone grasped her upper arm and steadied her.

She tossed her head back and looked upward into familiar dark green eyes. "Chase." She smiled with uncertainty. His rain-fresh scent swirled around her.

He lifted his cap off his head and tugged it back on. "How's the foot?" he asked, glancing around.

Camara panned the area to see what he

was looking for and wondered what had him so jittery. Not seeing anything out of the ordinary, she responded, "Fine. I'm getting around much better."

"You driving today?" His brows rose.

"No. Erik is."

"Oh."

She waited for him to say something else. When he didn't, she couldn't stand it any longer. Eyes downcast, she asked, "Chase, can we talk?" Camara peeked around. Two of the other drivers headed toward the booth. "Privately, please?"

He rubbed his forehead and eyes, saying nothing.

"Sorry." She shifted her crutches sideways, hopping on her left foot. "I know you need to register." As fast as she could, she scooted off. She recognized the sound of The Black Beast and figured Erik must be taking it off the trailer.

Chase fell in step beside her. Camara kept moving until Chase touched her arm. She stopped and looked up at him. Gazing into his emotionless eyes, Camara wanted to slink away. Where was the sweet man who had helped her so tenderly last Saturday? She must have been delusional and only imagined Chase being so thoughtful and caring.

"Cammy?" The deep softness in his voice didn't match his eyes. "I'm sorry. You said you wanted to talk. Let's go over there." He pointed to a wooden bench shaded by a large oak.

Camara maneuvered her way to the seat. Placing her crutches to the side, she stuck her foot out carefully. As she lowered herself down, Chase grabbed her arm and steadied her. She shifted her weight forward and cringed.

"You okay?"

No. But there was no way she was going to tell him she'd just taken a splinter in her backside. "Fine." She waved him off then glanced at her fidgety hands in her lap. "Look, I just wanted to tell you how much I appreciated everything you did for me."

"I'm glad I was able to help." With only his foot on the bench, Chase perused the area as if he were looking for something — or someone.

She grabbed her crutches and rose, placing them securely under her arms. "Well, I know you need to go get ready, so I won't keep you. Thank you." Hating feeling so vulnerable, Camara put her head down. "I don't know what I would have done if you hadn't come along." She peered up at him.

His green eyes softened, and his face

finally showed some emotion. He laid his warm calloused hand on her arm. "The thought of you being out there all alone —" His chest expanded, and he blew out a long breath. "Well, I'm glad you're okay." With that, and the barest of smiles, Chase stepped past her and walked away.

Camara didn't know what to think. One minute, Chase acted like he didn't want to be near her; then in the next, he acted like he truly cared about what happened to her.

The day and a half she had spent at the hospital nursing a concussion, Erik had told Camara repeatedly that Chase had changed since accepting Christ, but Camara still had a hard time believing it. She couldn't even trust her own assessment the night of the accident. Sure, it was true that Chase went with Erik to a men's fellowship breakfast every Thursday morning and to Wednesday's singles night and that they had become great friends . . . but Camara still couldn't bring herself to trust Chase. It was just too impossible to believe anybody could change that much.

CHAPTER 6

Chase leaned against the Mud Boss, which was parked about fifteen feet away from the orange fence barricade situated in front of the mud pits. He watched Erik get ready for a run.

"At pit number one is Tim Rosser, driving the Mud Hog, a '47 Willys Jeep with 38-inch Super Swampers, powered by a 350 engine.

"At pit number two, driving for Camara Cole, we have Erik Cole driving The Black Beast. . . ." The announcer's voice continued over the loudspeaker, but Chase's thoughts trailed to Cammy's beautiful face and those big brown eyes.

His heart had done funny things earlier when he'd run into her at the entry booth and she'd told him she didn't know what she would have done if he hadn't come along and helped her that night. That rare, vulnerable look on her face had almost caused him to pull her into his arms and kiss it away. That would have been a huge mistake. At that moment, he knew he had to get a grip on his growing feelings toward her. In the past, whenever Chase had dated a woman of whom his dad didn't approve, his father had made both their lives miserable. Chase couldn't let that happen to Camara. He'd just have to keep his distance from her. A heaviness settled into his stomach. *Lord, help me not to care for Camara.*

As soon as the prayer left his thoughts, he knew that was going to be impossible. Instead he had to figure out a way to break the control his dad had on his life — which wasn't going to be easy. Ever since he was a kid, his dad had controlled him. Whenever his father wanted his way, he made Chase's life miserable until he could no longer stand the pressure. Chase caved in to his father's demands every time. When he moved out of his parents' house, he thought the control and the need to win his dad's approval would vanish. But it hadn't. What constantly baffled Chase was that, even though he couldn't stand his dad's torturous treatment, he still loved him. Loved him enough to date the spoiled, highfalutin Brittany van Buran, with whom he had nothing in common. Dad approved of her because of her father's position — mayor of Swamper City. A long time ago Chase realized what he wanted and how he felt didn't matter to his dad. But at least he'd managed to untangle himself from Brittany . . . for now.

The loud roar of the trucks taking off in the mud pit drew his attention. Erik and Tim were even in the pit. At the sound of someone's screaming, Chase's gaze followed the noise until it landed on Camara. What a sight! Camara jumped up and down on her good leg while her crutches swung precariously outward at her sides. His heart leaped to his throat. Chase dropped his socket wrench and ran toward her.

Just as Erik pulled out of the mud pit barely ahead of Tim, she completely lost her balance. Thankfully, Chase caught her from behind. With his hands under her arms, she looked up at him and caught his gaze.

He steadied her as every emotion he tried to deny swept through him. Surprise bombarded him when she pivoted on her good foot then threw her arms around him.

"Did you see that? What a run!" Camara abruptly pulled away, glancing everywhere but at him. Her fingers dug into his arm as she struggled to keep her balance. "Where are my crutches?"

With one arm supporting her, he leaned over, picked up her crutches, and handed them to her.

Her gaze plummeted to the ground. "Thanks. Sorry I got carried away." She smiled sheepishly.

"I hadn't noticed." He started laughing. She shot him a mock sneer. It made him laugh harder. The sound of her beautiful laughter sang in his ears.

Erik pulled up in The Black Beast, and the fun moment dissipated. Her brother hopped out.

"Great job, bubba!" She gave him a high five.

"Thanks," he replied then glanced at Chase.

"How's it going?" Erik clasped Chase's hand.

"Pretty good," Chase answered. "Great run. Did you hear your time yet?"

"No, I missed it." Erik looked at Camara. "Did you hear it?"

"Um, no." She glanced at Chase and giggled.

Erik looked back and forth between them. "Did I miss something?"

"You mean you didn't see your sister? She started a new dance fad called the crutch swing."

Cammy wrinkled her pert nose at him.

"It's not safe to leave her alone, Erik. Well, gotta run. I'm up after these two." He glanced over at the Chevy Blazer and '79 Ford lined up at the pits.

"Talk to y'all later." He spun around but in the next heartbeat stopped dead in his tracks. Twenty feet away stood his dad with his arms crossed over his chest, glaring at him. Chase cringed. *Might as well get it over with,* he thought as he strode toward his dad.

Camara glanced past Chase to see why he'd stopped so suddenly. His dad scowled in their direction.

Camara licked her lips. Her mouth felt as dry as sand. She trudged her way toward the ice chest only a few yards from where Chase and his dad were. Shifting her crutches, she opened the lid.

"I'd better never see you talking to them Coles again, or I'll disown you. Not only that, I'll make sure the Coles regret the day they ever came near you. I told you before: Whatever you can do to destroy them Coles, do it. Is that understood?" Camara heard Chase's dad growl.

She didn't hear Chase's reply. Camara quickly snatched a Coke and quietly shut the lid. She moved away as fast as she could hobble. How sad that Chase's dad hated her family so much. And what did his dad mean that they'd be sorry? Whatever he meant, she didn't want to find out.

She rounded the corner of The Black Beast and met Chase's dad coming from the other direction. He glowered at her and hissed, "Stay away from my son." Her insides quivered at his toxic words and the evil in his eyes. "Or you'll be sorry," he spat. Then he stormed off.

Camara glanced at Chase, whose mouth was fixed in a straight line. His face was flushed, and the pained expression broke her heart. Now she understood why she hadn't heard from Chase and why he, too, had treated her so badly the last four years. It was because of his father's hatred toward her family. With a helpless shake of her head, she turned and started back to where Erik was hosing off The Black Beast.

Chase hated when his dad showed up at the mud bog races. He wished he would leave. He had never been so humiliated in his life. He wanted to dive into the mud and bury himself there. What must Camara think of him? Knowing his dad would stop at nothing to keep him away from her, Chase knew he needed to avoid her as much as possible and stop thinking about her.

After asking John what Erik's time was, Chase pulled himself up into his Ford Coupe, put on his helmet, and headed toward the pit. The rumbling in the cab pounded against his aching head. Normally he loved the powerful sound, but today the stress of his dad being there and the way he talked to Camara made his head throb.

Knowing he had to beat Erik's time or his dad would ream him, the pressure in his head intensified. He glanced at the other pit. Dave Marks's '78 Chevy Blazer, Time Bomb, rumbled. And although Chase knew his Coupe had enough power to beat Dave's, with the state of mind he was in, he wasn't sure he could beat anyone. He had to force himself to concentrate.

The flag dropped. Chase slammed the gas pedal to the floorboard. He dropped into the pit and took off, driving like a crazy man. It was as if he were pushing through his problems and burying them in his wake. He lunged up and out of the pit and glanced behind him. Dave's Blazer sat halfway through the pit. Chase drove to the contestants' pit, shut off his engine, and waited to see if he beat Erik's 11.7. He hated competing against his best friend. Erik had been nothing but good to him over the years.

Even before he was a Christian, Erik made it a point to talk to him. In a way, he wanted Erik to win. But knowing what his dad's response would be, Chase prayed that this time he'd win.

"Chase Lamar's time is 11.7. So far, we have a tie for first place between Erik Cole and Chase Lamar." Chase ignored the rest of the announcer's message and jumped out of his Coupe.

John gave him a high five. "Great job, buddy."

"Great job, my eyeball," his dad's gruff voice ground out. "You could have done better than that and showed up them Coles. Quit messing around and get out there and win."

Chase looked over his shoulder. John pointed toward the Mud Boss and the power sprayer and left.

Chase's heart nearly stopped. *Oh no!* Erik was heading his way with a big smile on his face. *God, please don't let Erik come over here. Please.*

"Hey, Chase. Great run. What'd ya do? Put wings under your hood? You flew through that pit." Erik clasped Chase's shoulder.

God, please don't let Dad say anything to humiliate me.

To his surprise and relief, his dad simply scowled and walked off to the side. Chase let out the breath he didn't know he'd been holding. "You had a good run, too."

"Oh, man. I forgot how much fun this was. I should build me another bogger." They both chuckled.

"Between running one of your dad's dealerships and building and racing monster trucks, when will you find the time to build a bogger?" Chase asked.

"Well, a guy can always dream, can't he? Besides, it would be odd competing against my baby sister. I could just hear her now."

Chase stuck his index finger in his ear and shook it. "Me, too. And it ain't a pretty sound."

They both burst out laughing.

It had been a long time since he'd had a good belly laugh.

"There's Stan," Erik said. "I'd love to chat, but I need to talk to him. I just came by to congratulate you and wish ya luck on your last run."

"You, too."

Erik turned and strode away. Over his shoulder he hollered, "May the best man win!"

"The best man will win," Chase's dad groused with a smirk on his face.

Something about the way his dad said those words caused a lump to settle in Chase's stomach. *Lord, I don't know what Dad meant by that, but please, keep Erik and Camara safe.*

CHAPTER 7

Camara popped the last french fry into her mouth. She maneuvered her crutches on the loose gravel as she headed toward Erik, who had just hopped into The Black Beast. Up next was the tiebreaker between Chase and Erik.

"Don't forget, bubba. Flip the NOS switch this time — right before the flag drops and —"

"Sis!" Erik cut her off and shot her a "That's enough!" look.

"Okay, okay. But your last run, you forgot to turn it on. You would have beat Chase's time by a good couple of seconds if you would have run the NOS."

"You wanna drive?"

Camara dropped her head. "No. Sorry."

"Look, I'm sorry I forgot to turn on the nitrous. I know how much winning this race means to you. I won't forget this time."

"Thanks, bubba." She backed away and

worked her way to the guardrail.

"Hey, sis."

Camara turned. "Tony! Where ya been?"

"Workin'. What else?"

Camara eyed him warily.

"Okay, okay. After Dad had me putting in sixty-plus-hour weeks for the last seven months, I took a minivacation and went fishin'. Another bass tournament." A grin stretched across his face. "Caught a four-pounder. And I got my barbecue all ready and waiting for ya at my house. I told the wife I was certain I could talk ya into grilling it for me."

Wrinkling her nose, Camara narrowed her brows. "Yeah, right. In your dreams. I wouldn't touch the slimy thing."

"You blow me away. You play in the mud in them there trucks, but you won't touch a fish?" He chuckled at her expression. "You know I'm teasing you, sis. Besides, the fish is being mounted." He hiked his foot on the guardrail. "So, what'd I miss?"

"C'mon. You're just in time to watch the tiebreaker between Chase and Erik." Over the loudspeaker, Camara heard The Black Beast and the Mud Boss lining up at the pits. Camara's finely tuned ear honed in to the sound of her engine. It wasn't running right. "Oh no. Not now."

"What's wrong?" Tony asked.

"Can't you hear it?"

"Hear what? It's so loud you can't hear anything but the trucks."

"The engine's missing — the spark plugs aren't firing right. I don't understand. It was running great awhile ago."

Unfortunately it was too late to do anything about her engine now. The flagger dropped the red flag. The Black Beast dove into the mud pit before the Mud Boss.

Camara held her breath. Halfway through the pit, The Black Beast bogged down. The more rpms Erik poured into it, the more the engine sputtered.

Chase leaped out of the pit.

The crowd roared.

The announcer's voice reverberated throughout the area. "Chase Lamar's time is 10.99." The announcer continued talking, but Camara tuned him out.

She couldn't wait until Erik brought her truck back so she could check it out. Crutches or no crutches, she'd figure out a way.

Tony beat her to her truck. By the time she hobbled to it, Erik had the hood raised and was leaning over the engine.

Camara hobbled next to them. "Tony, would you get my stand, please?"

"You'll get all muddy."

"I don't care. Please?"

Tony quickly retrieved her stepladder.

"Find anything, Erik?" Waiting impatiently on the ground caused her insides to jiggle.

"I'm just taking off the filter now so I can check the carburetor out. I don't get it. It ran fine earlier."

"Let me up there. I wanna check something. I think I know what's wrong."

Tony placed the stepladder in front of her. Camara crooked her bad ankle upward and leaned her crutches against the truck. Tony clutched her waist and hoisted her onto the top step, making sure she had her balance before letting go. "Tony, would you mind grabbing a plastic cup out of my Hummer, please?"

Tony headed toward her vehicle. Her brothers knew that once she got something on her mind, she went for it. No crutches would stop her. Camara unplugged the hose from the carburetor and manually pumped some fuel into the cup.

Several minutes later, the fuel settled. "I knew it."

"You knew what?" Tony and Erik asked.

"There's water in the fuel." She'd seen this enough times; she knew before she ever got under the hood what was wrong.

Erik's forehead creased. "How'd water get in the fuel cell? I filled it this morning myself. And I know the racing fuel was good then."

"Tony, will you help me down, please?"

Tony lowered her to the ground and handed her the crutches.

When she looked over at Chase and his dad, she thought they both looked rather pleased. Surely Chase wasn't so desperate to win that he would stoop so low as to sabotage her truck?

Earlier, when Erik had gone over to congratulate Chase and then talk to Stan, she'd gone to the restroom. Camara decided to see if Lolly noticed anyone hanging around the Beast.

"I need to drain the tank."

"I'll do it," Erik said.

"Thanks, bubba. I'll be right back."

"Where ya going?"

"To check on something."

She hobbled across the contestant's pit. "Hey, Stanley. I'd high-five ya, but with these crutches, I'd fall," she teased the lithe, six-foot-two man.

"Please don't. I don't wanna catch ya. Ya ain't big as a minute. I'd have to stoop too low for such a shrimp like you that I might hurt myself." He chortled, his blue eyes

91

sparkling with mischief.

Camara feigned a scowl. "Oh, go play in traffic. Just cuz you're a corn-king giant." She wrinkled her nose at him.

"Well, it's better than being a baby-pea-pod. Or Little Miss Shrimput who sat on her truckut." His lips twitched with mirth.

"That was *so* bad, Stan."

He raised a palm upward. "Hey, what can I say? I tried."

Camara glanced around. "Where's Lolly? I need to talk to her."

"What?" He held his hand over his heart. "You mean you didn't come over here to see me and declare your undying love for me?"

She giggled. "You nut. I'm sure Lolly would appreciate that."

Lolly stepped from behind their blue Ford. With her finger on her lips as a *shush* sign, she walked stealthily and stood behind her husband. Camara suppressed the urge to laugh.

"She wouldn't have to know." He waggled his brows.

"Oh yes, I would." Lolly pinched his arm and walked around to face him.

"Ouch." Stan wrinkled his face and rubbed his arm. "She pinches like a goose."

Lolly scrunched her nose at him. "Well, if

you'd behave, I wouldn't pinch you at all."

Lolly gave Camara an awkward hug around the crutches. "Long time no see. Sorry I wasn't there to help you this past week."

"You were where you needed to be. Your sister Jenny needed your help with her new baby. How are they doing?"

"Really good. Little Tyler is so cute. After being around him, I want one now." She looked at Stan and winked.

"That can be arranged." Stan gave Lolly a loving look.

"Okay, you two lovebirds."

"Sorry, I got carried away." Lolly's voice held no apology. Her face turned serious. "I'm so glad you didn't get hurt worse than you did. I don't know what I would do without my best friend." Lolly leaned closer and examined Camara's stitched-up, jagged wound just below the brim of her cap. "Will you have a scar? How you doing? And what have you been doing besides playing in the ditches?"

"First things first." Camara leaned on her crutches and held up a finger. "One, I'm supposed to tell you that I came over here to declare my undying love for your husband."

"For this big burly guy? Consider it

declared. You can have him." She winked at Stan.

"Nah. I think I'll pass. He's too tall for me, and besides, he doesn't like us shorties. But thanks anyway."

Stan rolled his eyes while Camara and Lolly giggled.

Camara held up another finger. "Two, I'm doing really well." She popped up a third finger. "Three, the doctor doesn't think it will scar too badly." Camara jerked up a fourth finger. "And four, what I've been up to is only 5 feet 2 1/2 inches."

"Shrimp," Stan muttered.

Camara wrinkled her nose at him. "Jealous?"

His brows arched.

"Excuse us, Stan, I need to borrow your wife a second." Camara looped her arm in Lolly's. Looking at her crutches, she shrugged and let go.

"I'll be back in a second, sweetie," Lolly said.

Stan nodded and headed toward his bogger.

Camara panned the area. Keeping her voice down, she asked, "Did you notice anyone hanging around The Black Beast?"

"You mean besides the millions of spectators who had their noses under that hood of yours or the scads of people taking pictures?"

"Smart aleck." Camara tapped Lolly's arm and leaned closer. "I mean, did you see anything unusual?"

"Well, I'd call that bunch you work with unusual," Lolly teased. "But Bobby-Rae, Lem, and Tim are always hanging around your and everyone else's trucks."

"Would you be serious, please? Someone put water in The Black Beast's fuel cell."

"What?"

Camara's gaze jerked around. Stan peeked at her from under One Bad Mudder's hood.

"Shh."

"Sorry. Is that why it ran so poor today?"

Camara nodded.

"Wow. I'm sorry." Lolly's forehead wrinkled. "Let's see. The only other people I noticed were Dave Marks . . ."

One of her competitors.

". . . some kids . . ."

There were always kids hanging around.

". . . and Chase and his dad. But again, that isn't unusual. They hang around everyone's boggers." She eyed Camara. "You don't think one of them did it, do you?"

"I'm not sure."

"You know, it rained for about an hour during the night. Maybe the cap wasn't on, and it rained in it."

Camara shook her head. "No. Erik said he had it in the shop all night."

"Loll." Stan's voice broke through their conversation. "You ready to get something to eat? I'm hungry."

"I'd better go. But if I hear anything, I'll let you know."

"Thanks." They shared a quick hug.

"Bye, Stanley."

"Ya know, Camara, the way that Chevy of yours missed today, you might consider getting rid of that thing." He chuckled. "And leave the auto mechanics to us men."

"Stan! Stop it!" Lolly rebuked him.

He winked at Camara. "She knows I'm just teasing." He grabbed Lolly's hand and tugged her away. "Bye, shrimp."

Lolly looked over her shoulder and mouthed, "Sorry."

It was like being sucker punched. Although Stan was teasing her, it still hurt. Anytime one little thing went wrong, he'd tell her to get rid of her Chevy and leave the auto mechanics to the men. It seemed like no matter how hard she tried, it was never good enough. Guys still teased her and sometimes got downright cruel.

Dejected, Camara hobbled toward her truck.

Dave Marks stepped out from the side of his Chevy Blazer right in her path. Camara jerked to a stop, nearly falling. After gaining her balance, she looked at him and inwardly groaned. Dave stood almost eye level to her with his chest puffed out and his arms akimbo. He reminded her of a bantam rooster. She sighed heavily. Just what she needed — another harassing moron. Well, she refused to let him intimidate her. Camara looked him square in the eye.

His brown eyes dimmed. "I keep tryin' to tell ya to get rid of that piece of junk ya race. And," he added with a disgusting macho attitude and a spit of tobacco, "it's obvious by the way that Chevy of yours ran t'day that ya don't know what you're doin'." His snide, egotistical smile made her skin crawl.

Camara spun the bill of her cap around. *One . . . two . . .*

Dave raised his hands. "Hey, don't go blowin' a gasket on me. I'm only tryin' to help."

Yeah, right. And donkeys fly. And pigs swim. Three . . . four . . . five . . . Help me to control my anger, Jesus.

Besides, the only reason her truck ran so poorly today was because someone had sabotaged the fuel. But she didn't need to justify herself to him — or anyone else. If it took forever, she'd find out who did it. And she'd start with Chase Lamar and his father.

Camara tried hobbling around Dave, but he kept getting in her way.

"Ya need a man's help fixin' that thing."

Six . . . seven . . . Give me grace, Lord.

"Someone like me," he said, pointing to himself, "who knows what he's doin'."

He clutched her shoulders. Flames shot out from Camara's eyes. He was pushing it. She glared at him then flicked his hands off her shoulders. Dave grasped them again, sending pain racing down her arms. With his face mere inches from hers, his garlic and tobacco breath about bowled her over. Normally she liked the smell of grease and fuel, but the combination of them, the garlic, the tobacco, and the sweat turned her stomach. She tried pulling back, but he clenched her more firmly. *Eight . . . nine.* She reined in the urge to bop him with her crutch.

"I think we'd make a pretty good team." He looked at her mouth and licked his dry, chapped, tobacco-stained lips.

Ew, gross. Put those disgusting things anywhere near me, buster, and I'll belt ya one. Ten! "Oh, go play in traffic. You'd be the last person on earth I'd ever team up with.

Now, let me go, ya big bully!" She squirmed, trying to free herself from his strong grasp.

"I love a feisty woman." His hands gripped her even tighter, hurting her.

"Leave me alone!" Camara flipped her arm upward, trying to hit him with her crutch.

"You heard the lady. Let her go."

Camara jerked around as Chase came and stood next to her.

"I said, get your hands off her. . . . Now!" Chase's voice brooked no argument. He stood a good eight inches taller than Dave.

Dave's hands fell from her arms. "Cool your jets. I was just havin' some fun with her."

Camara leaned on her crutches and rubbed her aching arms.

With his fists clenched at his sides and the veins in his arms bulging, Chase got right in Dave's face. "You *ever* so much as even look at her again, you'll answer to me."

Dave backed away. "So, that's how it is," he drawled. "The two rivals are now lovers." He spun around. As he strutted away, he yelled over his shoulder, "You kin have her. I want a *real* lady."

Chase took a step toward Dave. Camara grabbed his arm and shook her head. Although Dave's words stung, she didn't want

Chase getting in a fight because of her.

She studied Chase's profile as he stared in the direction Dave headed. What kind of game was Chase playing anyway? Rescuing her one moment and possibly plotting with his dad to sabotage her truck the next. Was he messing with her mind or what? Why didn't he just do what his dad told him to do and leave her alone?

CHAPTER 8

Two weeks had passed since Chase's bitter victory. The trophy on the glass shelf mocked him. He was convinced if someone hadn't messed with The Black Beast, Erik would have won. Chase just hoped it wasn't who he thought had deliberately messed with it. Slinging himself from his mahogany leather couch, he hustled over to the trophy and snatched it up. In seven strides, he stormed into the kitchen and tossed it in the trash can.

He stomped back to the couch and plopped down. Dejected, he leaned forward, placed his elbows on his knees, and clasped his hands. "Lord, what am I gonna do? You command us to honor our father and mother, but Dad is so obsessed with beating the Coles, I think he's losing it. And, Lord, I really like Cammy, and I'd love to get to know her better. I wanna ask her out after the mud races next Saturday, but what if Dad finds out?" Chase pressed his hand over his face. "I hate feeling like I'm five years old again, needing permission to go play at a friend's house. But it's hard telling what Dad might do to me and to Camara if he found out. Since he booted Mom and Heather out, he's gotten worse.

"Father, please give me wisdom on how to handle this whole thing. It shouldn't even be an issue. I don't live at home, and yet Dad still controls my life. All I want to do is own a mechanic's shop and work on vehicles. But Dad insists I learn the business so I can take it over one day. Heather's begged Dad to let her run his companies after she graduates. She has a great head for business, but he refuses because she's female." He glanced skyward. "I know, I used to act that way, too. If only Dad would become a Christian, he would be happy." Chase paused. "Come to think of it, Lord, I don't think I've ever seen my dad happy." Chase released a long breath. "Lord, give me the grace to handle this. In Jesus' name, amen."

The heavy burden lifted. He was grateful John had been persistent and that he'd found Jesus. Now, if only God could get ahold of his dad.

Chase glanced at his watch: seven thirty

p.m. Maybe Pastor Stephans was home. He'd been so busy the last two weeks he hadn't had a chance to call and make an appointment. Chase picked up his phone and dialed the number.

After making a lunch appointment for the following afternoon, Chase looked around his lavish house. The circular mahogany couch with the matching love seat and recliner barely made a dent in the space of the large room. Chase hated the abstract pictures on the walls. He preferred a more rustic look. The only part of this house that represented him was the den that sported his trophies and collector model cars. His father had insisted on hiring a famous decorator to furnish the place. His mother had offered to help, but his father refused. Chase wondered if he'd ever get up enough guts to break free from his father's domineering personality.

His dad believed money bought happiness. Well, the plantation-style mansion with its lavish furnishings hadn't made his dad happy. The old adage about money can't buy happiness . . . his dad was living proof of that. And so was Chase until a few months ago when he'd given his life to the Lord and found the true source of happiness. If only his dad understood that true fulfillment comes from a relationship with Jesus Christ.

Chase ran his hand over his spiked hair. He needed answers from Pastor Stephans on how to break free from his dad's controlling powers and yet still honor him as the Bible commanded. Plus, he needed wisdom on how to deal with his dad's destructive attitude, and he needed them before his dad did something everyone would regret. Especially him.

After showering, Chase pulled on a pair of neatly pressed jeans, brown suede loafers, and a light pink shirt. He checked himself in the mirror and decided he would be presentable for his luncheon engagement with Pastor Stephans after church this morning. Chase gathered his keys and headed toward church.

Spotting a couple of empty parking places, he parked his truck and got out. Several maple, pine, and Bradford pear trees shaded the back of the parking lot. But because the Alabama sun was so hot, the shade didn't help ward off the heat. Chase wiped the sweat off his forehead and glanced at the large A-frame church. Prisms of light danced off the three stained-glass windows. Camellia, the reddish-pink Alabama state flower, lined the front of the white building, giving Chase a small glimpse of heaven's brilliance. Camara pulled her Hummer into the spot next to him.

When she stepped out, Chase's breath vanished. She looked amazing in the blue floral summer dress that flowed to her calves. A few strands of her blond hair blew across her cheeks. It took every bit of self-control he possessed to keep his hand from reaching out to move the wayward strands from her face. Her tanned skin made her brown eyes look like creamy hot fudge topping. A pink hue fanned the scar on her forehead.

"Um, uh." Camara cleared her throat.

Chase felt heat start from his stomach and end up in his cheeks. "Good morning." He fought to mask his embarrassment. "What, no crutches?"

"Good morning to you, too. My ankle's doing much better." Her bright reply surprised and delighted him. He wasn't sure how she would act toward him after the way his dad had spoken to her.

"It's late. We'd better hurry. Race ya." She sent him an ornery look and took off running.

Chase stared after her. Her sandals slapped against the asphalt. He noticed she favored her sore foot. Not about to be outdone, he darted after her. Only two feet separated them. Chase changed his mind and deliberately slowed his pace so Camara would win.

Camara stopped at the steps and swirled around. "Told ya," she said breathlessly. Giving him a smug look, she threw her shoulders back, clutched her compact Bible to her chest, and strode up the steps still limping generously on her hurt ankle. Nothing seemed to stop Camara. Chase smiled and shook his head. She was some kind of woman. His kind, to be exact.

On his way up the steps, he overheard an elderly woman speaking to the gray-haired gentleman whose arm she clutched. "Oh, Donald. Don't they make the cutest couple? He must love her dearly. When we were young, you used to let me win, too."

Chase swallowed back his embarrassment at the lady's remark. He quickly glanced to see if Camara had heard. If she did, she didn't let on. She just kept walking toward the door. That lady didn't know what she was talking about. He didn't love Camara. He liked her a lot, and she consumed his every thought lately, but love? Shaking the absurd thought from his brain, Chase made his way toward the double doors.

■ ■ ■ ■

Camara had felt pretty smug about winning until she heard an elderly lady say something about Chase letting her win because he loved her. Obviously that lady didn't know what she was talking about. Chase had never *let* anyone beat him at anything, especially Camara. They'd been rivals too long. Rivals who loved goading each other. Sure, things were different between them since her accident. She now noticed his good looks, handsome smile, and physique that even a bodybuilder would envy.

When she reached for the church door handle, Chase's hand landed on top of hers. She peered up at him. His warm, rough hand melted her insides. Moving ceased to be important. Someone behind them cleared their throat. Camara blinked. Her cheeks flamed.

"Let me get that." A slow, knowing smile spread across Chase's face.

She jerked her hand out from under his and looked away. "Thanks."

Chase opened the door and motioned her ahead of him.

Peppy praise music greeted her. Not wanting to walk down the long aisle late, she

107

spotted a seat in the back row clear against the far wall.

She limped over and politely asked the middle-aged man if he would move over a bit. He smiled and scooted down the pew. Setting her Bible on the seat, she started clapping and singing.

A slight nudge on her shoulder made her look sideways. Chase motioned for her to scoot over.

Her eyebrows shot upward. There really wasn't enough room for him. She glanced at the man next to her, and as if he knew, he scooted over as far as she thought he could.

Chase's presence filled the end of the row. There wasn't any extra room between her and the man next to her. Not wanting to be rude by crowding the gentleman, she had no choice but to allow Chase's arm to press tightly against hers.

The touch sent a foreign, tingling sensation throughout her arm.

She darted a quick glance at him and wondered if he felt it, too. By his stunned expression, he must have.

Their gazes locked, and the air evaporated from the room. The next song started, and Chase broke the connection. Camara swallowed. What had come over her? This was

Chase. Chase Lamar . . . her longtime rival. *Get a grip, Cam.*

Chase's deep baritone voice disrupted her thoughts. Forgetting everything for a moment, Camara focused on the two men standing on either side of her who were praising God in perfect harmony. The bass voice of the man next to her mingling with Chase's baritone sent chills all over her body. She closed her eyes and let the wonderful presence of God wash over her. *Oh, Lord, I love You. I'm so grateful to know You as my Lord and Savior. Thank You for the privilege of being in Your house. You're so wonderful, Lord.*

Several songs later, she glanced at Chase. Eyes closed, face tilted heavenward, light seemed to radiate around him. She'd never witnessed a more beautiful sight. Mesmerized, Camara stared at him.

Was this the same man she'd been rivals with? The same man who had mercilessly tormented her for being a Chevy lover, a mud bog racer, and the forbidden female mechanic? This Chase loved God and wasn't afraid to show it. This man glowed from within. And this man, if she wasn't careful, could easily capture her heart.

As Chase sang, unchecked tears trickled

down his face. He silently praised God for His loving-kindness, His mercy, His grace, His peace, but most of all for allowing a man such as himself to find God's forgiveness through Jesus Christ. What an amazing, loving heavenly Father Chase served.

Chase thought about his own father. Heaviness shrouded his heart.

Oh, Jesus, if only Dad knew how wonderful You really are. Then he would understand why I love You so much and why I won't give You up. Chase swiped away his tears. *Since Mom became a Christian and no longer cares about worldly things, I think it makes Dad feel like he isn't needed anymore. He sure has changed since he drove out Mom and Heather. In fact, he's become so mean he's starting to do things that border on being dangerously illegal.*

Camara stirred next to him. The smell of her sweet gardenia perfume permeated the air.

Lord, I'm afraid for Camara. I have this feeling that my father will follow through with his threat toward her.

Feeling a need to connect with her, keeping his eyes closed, Chase clasped Camara's hand. *Keep her safe, Lord. And help my father to know You.*

When the music had stopped, Chase

wasn't certain. He opened his eyes and found Camara staring at him. Then she looked down at their clasped hands and hiked both brows. Chase smiled and reluctantly let go. He opened his mouth to say something, but Pastor Stephans walked up to the podium, asked them to be seated, and started his sermon.

Chase didn't hear a word he said. His mind stayed on Camara. Why had he never seen how truly lovely she was . . . inside and out?

CHAPTER 9

Camara leaned against her Hummer and watched the entrance to Swamper Speedway, waiting for Chase to arrive. Ever since church last Sunday, she viewed Chase in a whole new light.

During worship when Chase had held her hand, she was completely taken aback. When she looked over at him and noticed the tears trailing down his cheeks and his face glowing with peacefulness, her heart had softened instantly toward him.

The familiar sound of his diesel pickup drew her attention. Chase pulled his pickup and trailer alongside hers.

Camara couldn't control her rapid-firing pulse.

Chase stepped out of his pickup, walked over to her, and gave her a quick hug. She eyed him suspiciously. She wanted to know who this man was and what he did with the old Chase.

He laid his hand on her arm, causing a tremor to shimmy up her arm. Not used to her new feelings toward him, she didn't know how to act.

He smiled, and her breath caught in her throat. Why hadn't she appreciated how truly handsome he was before?

Chase looked over her head, and his smile vanished. Camara turned around to see what had wiped the smile off his face.

Chase's dad was driving toward them. Remembering his threat, Camara said, "I gotta go get ready." Never one to back away from a challenge, for Chase's sake, Camara turned and sprinted around the back of her trailer. Because of Mr. Lamar's hatred toward her family, she knew there could never be anything between her and Chase. Not even friendship. His dad would see to that. Besides, she didn't want anything coming between Chase and his dad — especially her. All things considered, Camara decided it would be best to just stay clear of Chase.

Unsnapping the straps from The Black Beast, she felt someone tap her shoulder. Camara spun around.

"Ya need some help?"

"What do you want?" Camara asked, narrowing her gaze at the grease-stained mountain sporting a red T-shirt minus the sleeves.

"Well now, I figured I'd been so awful to you that I'd make it up to ya by seeing if ya needed any help." Bobby-Rae's smile didn't quite reach his eyes.

Camara scrunched her face. Why would he offer to help her when he barely talked to her lately, and the last time he had, he'd insulted her so badly? She had a feeling he was up to no good.

"Hey, what's up?" Camara heard Chase's voice behind her. She watched Chase step forward, relieved that he'd interrupted them.

"That offer stands," Bobby-Rae said to Camara. Looking at Chase, he turned and stalked off.

Judging from his hasty departure, Camara assumed Bobby-Rae didn't want to tangle with Chase. Not that she blamed him. Chase was a stout man whose quickness and skill during fights had earned him a reputation as someone not to mess with. Now she had another Chase-saving-her-skin story to tell Lolly. If she wasn't careful, she might end up with a whole bunch of them, the way this was going. Stifling the thought and a giggle, she turned to him.

"Did you want something?"

"I was just passing by and thought I'd say hi." He sent her a look she couldn't quite decipher.

Disappointed, she plastered on a fake smile. "Okay," she said, forcing a lightheartededness into her voice. One she didn't feel. "See ya at the pit."

When Chase made no effort to leave, she sent him a questioning look.

"Actually" — he raised his Ford cap and tugged it back on his head — "I came by to see if you would have lunch with me today."

Camara tilted her head, studying Chase's face to see if he was serious. Unable to discern if he was or not, she said, "You and me" — pointing between herself and him — "have lunch together?" She chuckled nervously. "That's funny, Chase."

Chase's features went from chipper to crushed. "I'm serious. Would you like to have lunch with me?"

She started to say yes until she caught a glimpse of his dad standing several yards away from them, scowling at her.

"Maybe some other time, okay? I can't today."

"Some other time then." He tipped his cap, turned, and left.

She watched Chase meander toward his father. The two of them talked then looked toward her. Something about that whole scene made Camara uneasy.

Erik pulled up next to Camara in his semi-tractor trailer loaded with his monster truck. With his elbow resting against the door, he leaned his head out the window. "Hey, sis," Erik said over the loud *crr crr crr crr* of his diesel engine. "I'll park this thing and then come help ya."

While they unloaded The Black Beast from the trailer, Camara told Erik about Bobby-Rae's offer to help.

"I thought he was mad at you."

"Me, too." She shrugged. "Oh well. It's Bobby-Rae. Who ever knows what he's thinking."

A deep voice came over the loudspeaker announcing it was time to start signing up for the day's events. Camara headed that way.

Chase walked in step beside her. "Mind if I walk with you?"

She darted a glance at him. "Won't your dad mind?"

He laid his hand on her arm and stopped her. "Listen, Cammy. I know what Dad said to you. But that's how he feels. It's not how I feel. I'll deal with my dad."

"Chase." She gently removed his hand. "I don't think it's wise if we talk. Your dad hates us, and I don't want there to be any more problems between us. We've just

116

started becoming friends. Let's keep it that way." She looked up at him and caught his gaze. Willing him to understand, she added, "Better make that distant friends." Camara quickly trotted toward the entry booth.

While Camara stood in line, Chase walked up next to her and whispered in her ear, "No. Not distant friends. I want more," he said then moved into the other line.

Camara's heart revved up. She didn't know what to think of Chase's newfound interest in her.

After they attached the cable to the rear receiver hitch of her truck, Camara lined up at the pit. Next to her was Ben Sands, driving his silver Chevy Cameo pickup, the Mud Slinger. This was the last race of the day. In order to win today's race, she had to beat Chase's time of 10.72.

The flagman raised the flag.

With shaky hands, Camara pushed the master switch, turning on her NOS. She put her left foot on the brake and pressed her right foot on the gas.

The flag dropped.

Camara jerked her left foot off the brake and floored the gas pedal. The Black Beast lunged forward ahead of Ben. Halfway through the pit, right before she was ready to engage the NOS, her truck started sputtering, slowing her pace. Camara watched Ben pass her and lunge up and out of the mud pit. Turning her wheels to the right, then to the left, The Black Beast bogged down in the thick mire with her engine not running right. "Oh, man!" Camara slammed her hands against the steering wheel. What had gone wrong? Everything was running fine when she checked it before leaving the shop this morning.

Camara flipped the NOS switch off. She wanted to hide her face while they pulled her out of the pit. Despair and anger wrapped around her as she realized Chase had won again. Now he was ahead of her by two races.

Camara's truck jerked and sputtered as she made her way toward the contestants' pit.

Erik met her and swung open her door. "What went wrong? It sounds terrible."

"I don't know." She flipped all the toggle switches off, shutting off the pickup.

She hopped out, ran around to the passenger side, and grabbed her stepladder. Camara placed the ladder near the front fender of the truck and stepped up.

"What happened out there?"

With a close of her eyes to rein in her

anger, she groaned at the sound of Chase's voice. Opening her eyes, she studied his face to see if there was any sign of gloating. However, what she saw was worse. Pity. Well, she didn't need or want his sympathy. Right now she only wanted to find out why her truck ran so rough. "I don't know, but I'm fixin' to find out. Now if you'll excuse me."

Doing her best to ignore him and everything else, she popped the hood open. From the corner of her eye, she noticed him turn to leave. *Good.*

Her brother leaned over the hood as she checked through the system. Everything seemed to be fine. She stepped down and walked to the back of the truck. In one instant, she saw the problem — fuel dripping from the fuel cell exit line.

A sick thudding feeling pitted Camara's stomach.

"Erik, look at this." The hose clamp was loosened enough on the fuel line that it had caused it to suck in air.

Erik examined the clamp. "How'd that happen?"

She had her suspicions but didn't voice them. The only time her truck had been unattended was when she and Erik had gone to grab a barbecue sandwich. Maybe

119

the fiend did it then. Surely he wasn't so desperate to win that he would do such a thing to her. Would he?

During the next two weeks, Camara and Erik watched The Black Beast at every conceivable moment. She'd won both races since then, and now she and Chase were tied in points. Not wanting to risk losing, she vowed to continue watching The Black Beast like a hawk.

"Hi, Cammy." Chase's deep drawl broke through her thoughts. "Erik." Chase reached for Erik's hand and shook it.

She'd been avoiding Chase like a bad virus. She glanced up to find both Erik and Chase staring at her. Did she have food on her face or something? She self-consciously wiped at her mouth. "What?" she asked them. "What are y'all looking at me like that for?"

It was clear neither one wanted to be the one to start. With a glance at Chase, Erik took the dive. "Well, sis. Chase and I've been talking."

Uh-oh. She raised her brows. "About what?" she asked, not really wanting to know. She took a sip of her sweetened tea.

"About you."

She hiked a brow. "What about me?"

"Well . . ." Erik shifted his weight back and forth. A sure sign he was up to something she wouldn't like. She knew that look in his eyes. He was pleading with her to understand. "The church needs a new roof. And, well . . ." Erik glanced at Chase and then back at her. "Chase and I thought about a fund-raiser."

Camara frowned. Not really wanting to ask but wanting to know what the two of them were up to, she drew in a deep breath and asked, "What kind of fund-raiser?"

"We've already talked to Pete, and he said we could use Pete's Mud-n-Track to have a mud bog race."

Camara let out the breath she'd been holding. "Oh . . . is that all?"

"No, there's more," Chase chimed in. "Erik was so sure you'd win that I challenged him."

"That challenge includes you," Erik added sheepishly.

"Me?" She tilted her head. "What's this challenge involve, anyway?" She darted a quick glare her brother's way.

"If you win, I have to wear a Chevy-lover jacket the rest of the mud bog racing season."

"You?" Camara hooted.

Nodding, Chase grimaced. "But if I win,

you have to agree to spend a whole day with me."

"What?" Camara's mouth dropped open. She whirled her gaze toward her brother. "Are you crazy? Me and *him?* On a date?" she shrieked and shook her head furiously. "Y'all have been smelling too many gas fumes." She sent Erik a how-could-you? look.

"What? You afraid of losing?" Chase challenged.

Camara scrunched her face and stared hard at him. "Lose to *you?*" She tucked her hair behind her ears. "I have only one thing to say. . . . Name the day and time, and I'll be there."

CHAPTER 10

What had Camara gotten herself into? How was she supposed to know Chase had installed nitrous oxide in his '34 Ford Coupe prior to the fund-raiser? She'd been so certain she'd win that she really hadn't thought about the ramifications of accepting the challenge. Camara sighed heavily. If only he'd lost. She giggled just thinking about him having to wear a Chevy-lover jacket at the mud bog races. That would have been one for the history books.

Camara pulled on white shorts with her favorite flower, yellow daisies, on the bottom left side. Her blouse had the same print on the right side near her shoulder. She slipped on her white sandals with tiny yellow daisies across the strap and buckled them. Checking herself in the mirror one last time, she shook her head. Never before had she worn so many cute outfits and dresses as she had this summer. Today, for some odd reason, she wanted to look her best for her date with Chase. Who would have ever thought she, Camara Cole, would be going on a date with Chase Lamar? Stranger things had happened, she supposed.

She started wondering about where he might take her. She'd always wanted to go to Noccalula Falls Park in Gadsden to see the statue of the legendary Indian chief's daughter, Noccalula, who chose to jump off the falls rather than marry the man she didn't love. That was where Slick took his last date, and it sounded romantic. And last summer Lolly couldn't stop talking about the Gilliland-Reese Covered Bridge at Noccalula. That sounded romantic, too. Then again, Lolly had a way of romanticizing anything she and Stan did together. Camara readjusted her top. Well, maybe Chase would take her to the botanical gardens there or on the nature trails. She glanced at her sandals. If he did that, she'd have to change shoes. For a split second she considered changing them but decided that was a dumb idea, since she didn't even know where they were going.

In fact, knowing her luck, Chase would probably be ornery enough to take her coon hunting. Or even worse, drive hours to Tuscumbia to the Key Underwood Coon Dog Memorial Graveyard or take her bass fishing. Camara shuddered as the options got worse. She hated fishing and hunting of any kind. That's where her girlie side kicked in. What the local guys got out of killing animals was beyond her comprehension. Many more even less intriguing possibilities spiraled through her mind. She stared in the mirror and wondered what had possessed her to go ahead with this date in the first place. Because she trusted Erik's judgment, that's why. Camara found herself actually looking forward to today, providing there were no coons, fish, or dead deer in sight.

The doorbell rang. Camara's stomach fluttered. She skipped down the steps.

Chase rang Camara's doorbell, drew in several long breaths, and exhaled slowly. Uncertain of the reception he'd receive, he fumbled for a breath mint and popped it into his mouth. He couldn't believe how jittery his insides were. It wasn't like this was his first date. He'd dated plenty. But this date was different. Camara had been hoodwinked into it.

It seemed like he'd waited a lifetime to spend a day alone with Camara. He wanted to get to know the real her — the other part of her, aside from the competitive, maniacal, racer-mechanic he'd butted heads with the last four years.

The door opened. His eyes widened as he drank in the sight of her. Standing in front of him was a very feminine, beautiful woman. Each time he saw her dressed like a lady instead of a grease monkey, he wanted to ask why she didn't let the world see her like this more often. But each time, he held his tongue, not wanting to rile her.

"Hi, Chase, come on in. I'll just be a minute." She moved out of the way and let him enter. When he walked past her, he caught a whiff of soap and spring flowers.

"Is there anything I need to bring?" She tilted her head. The way her hair fell across her eye did strange things to his insides. He wanted to reach out and move it away then run his finger over her soft cheek. His gaze went to her mouth.

"Chase? Did you hear me?"

Heat rose to his cheeks. He couldn't believe he was blushing. His buddies would never believe it, and he wasn't going to be the one to tell them.

The amused look on her face made him want to run out the door. But no way would he miss his chance to finally go out with her.

He pulled himself together. "You'll need to bring a light jacket and a swimsuit."

"Oh? Where are we going?"

"You'll just have to wait and see." He smirked.

She looked adorable the way she wrinkled her pert nose at him. He couldn't wait to get to know the real Cammy — the feminine Camara standing in front of him. He also hoped they could put their differences aside and get to know each other for who they really were — not just competitors at the pits.

"I'll grab my things." She turned and sashayed toward the stairs.

Chase glanced around her bright living room. On his left was a fireplace with a round oak table between two overstuffed couches. A sycamore table sat in front of the wall-to-wall sliding glass windows. He could see out into her yard, where he noticed a large rock fountain in the center of a well-manicured lawn lined with yellow daisies. When he heard a door shut upstairs, his gaze drifted that way. Along one wall near the stairs was a floor-to-ceiling glass and brass bookshelf with trophies and classic model cars. Plus several replicas of famous monster trucks. The shelf reminded him of his.

"Okay." She grabbed a lined Windbreaker and keys and shoved them in her yellow duffel bag. "I'm ready."

She might be ready, but was he?

To protect her shorts-clad legs from the hot leather seat, Camara spread a beach towel over one of the front bench seats on the pontoon boat. She couldn't take her gaze off Chase sitting behind the wheel. While he paid close attention to navigating the boat, she imagined the deep concentration in those dark green eyes hidden behind those black sunglasses. Eyes that earlier had stared at her when he'd first arrived at her house. She stifled a giggle.

He'd looked so cute standing there speechless and blushing. That was another side of Chase she'd never seen before. And one she found extremely attractive. Her heart did a funny little dance.

Her gaze shifted to the bronze skin of his arms. She glanced at her lightly tanned legs and was envious of him. Reaching inside her duffel bag, she grabbed the suntan lotion with bug protection and started rubbing it on her legs, arms, and face; then she tossed it back in her bag. Perfumed coconut lingered in the air. Mosquitoes buzzed around her but didn't land. The cool, refreshing spray of the water was a reprieve from the ninety-degree weather.

As they traveled across Lake Guntersville, the beautiful lake nestled in the Appalachian Mountain foothills, Camara marveled at how many tiny islands there were. Lush trees lined the shore in some areas, while others were dotted with tall, spindly trees and geese. Several mansions spread along the winding shoreline. Camara sniffed the air. The sweet smell of coral honeysuckle and magnolias wafted around her.

Along the way, Camara returned the friendly waves of people on their houseboats near the bank.

Leaning back on her hands, she closed her eyes and enjoyed the hot sun on her body and face. She was so glad Chase brought her to this fantastic place.

"Dollar for your thoughts?"

Camara's eyes opened. She turned her face toward him.

"I was thinking about you."

He dipped his head, lowered his sunglasses on his nose, and peered over the dark rims. "Oh yeah?"

"Yeah." She paused, wondering how much she should tell him. "I was thinking about how much you've changed."

"Oh." He sounded disappointed as he pushed his sunglasses back in place. "In what way?"

"Well" — she swiped a tiny bug off her leg — "I was thinking about the day Erik told me you'd accepted the Lord. I didn't believe it." She glanced at a sailboat passing by and returned the passengers' wave then looked back at Chase. "When I saw you in church several weeks ago" — she placed her bare feet on the carpeted boat floor, facing him — "you had tears flowing down your face, and you glowed. I knew your conversion was real because the Chase I knew was so busy being Mr. Macho that he wouldn't have let anyone see him cry."

She wished he'd take off his sunglasses. It had been said the eyes were the mirror of the soul, and she'd love to get a good glimpse into his soul right now.

"I can see why you didn't believe him. I was pretty mean . . . especially to you." He slowed the boat down and turned sideways in his seat. Even though he had sunglasses on, his head was bowed so she knew he was looking at the seat rather than her. "Look, I want you to know I'm sorry for the things I've said and done to you. If you wanna know the truth . . . I was . . ." He removed his sunglasses and caught her gaze. "I was jealous of you." He quickly replaced his sunglasses, but not before Camara glimpsed the sincerity in his eyes.

"Why would you be jealous of me?"

"Because of your family's close relationship."

"Oh," she said, keeping the disappointment out of her voice. She secretly hoped it was because of her racing and mechanical abilities.

Chase looked forward and then turned the steering wheel left. "I've always wanted a close relationship with my father, but he's too busy trying to make money and thinking of new ways to outsell your dad." He killed the engine and looked at her. "Dad believes that whenever he takes business away from your father, he's somehow getting revenge for what happened in the past. For years, my mom told him what your dad did was an accident and that he needed to let it go because it was eating him alive. But her words only led to a massive fight. He said it would be over his dead body before he forgave that —" Chase suddenly stopped and smiled sheepishly. "It's still hard to believe they were best friends from sixth grade until their senior year in college."

Camara pursed her lips and nodded.

A shadow covered the boat. A strong wind

131

whipped her hair across her face. She glanced up at the sky. Chase followed her gaze. They'd been so intent on their conversation, they hadn't noticed the dark clouds rolling in.

Chase started the boat and shoved a lever forward. The boat picked up speed as they headed toward the shore.

"Where are we going?"

"To my family's vacation house."

Camara's eyes darted open. How could he take her to his family's vacation house? What if his dad showed up there? After all, the man seemed to show up everywhere else. . . . She knew she shouldn't have trusted Chase. She never should have accepted that stupid challenge in the first place. But then again, if she hadn't, Chase would have believed it was because she thought he would win. *Ack!* She could boot herself in the backside for reneging on her vow not to trust him. If nothing else, she should have at least gotten involved in planning this date.

"Don't panic." His smile did nothing to reassure her. "My dad is out of town on business until Tuesday. Or otherwise I wouldn't risk taking you there."

Camara's mouth slackened. Had he just read her mind?

Lightning cracked across the sky like a jagged scar. A loud boom immediately followed, raising the hair on her arms. Camara squealed. She quickly gathered her things and moved to the seat directly behind Chase so she could be under the canopy.

"Grab a couple of life jackets from under that seat," Chase ordered.

Against the rocking movement of the boat, Camara struggled to balance herself while she retrieved a couple of jackets from the storage unit under the seat. She let the lid slam shut. After handing Chase a jacket, she quickly slid into hers and fastened the three straps. Plopping herself down, she grabbed hold of the railing and hung on for dear life.

Water sprayed her face as small waves splashed over the boat. Camara scanned the area. Black, threatening clouds loomed over the rolling landscape as far as she could see. In a breath, heavy sideways rain started pelting her skin. She picked up her duffel bag, grabbed her Windbreaker from it, and tried putting it on, but it was too small to fit over the life jacket. She hurried to remove the jacket; then she put on her Windbreaker and the life jacket over it.

When she looked ahead, she saw a large plantation-style house not too far away. "Is that it?"

"Yes."

"God, please help us make it there," she whispered, knowing how vicious these Appalachian storms could be. Her heart slammed against her ribs as fast as the waves were beating against the boat. Was it her imagination, or was the boat no longer moving forward?

"Chase? Are we gonna make it?" She couldn't keep the quiver from her voice.

"We need to get this boat docked as soon as possible and get inside before . . ." He looked toward the sky. "Before the hail hits."

Camara watched Chase struggling to keep the boat heading toward the house. Camara relaxed a bit. They were only feet from the dock.

"Hold on, Camara. The way the waves are, it might be pretty rough." Chase's voice boomed over the loud thunder.

Lightning pierced the sky again. Camara closed her eyes. *Lord, please help Chase get the boat docked. And keep us safe.* She opened her eyes.

As Chase maneuvered the vessel alongside the private dock, a large wave pushed the pontoon boat, slamming it against the dock. Camara hoped the padded sides would keep the boat from getting dented.

"Wait here." Chase anchored both ends of the boat and ran back to her. "C'mon, we've got to hurry and get to the house."

Before Camara had a chance to even respond, Chase grabbed her hand and helped her out of the boat and onto a wooden walkway.

"We'll have to make a run for the house."

The wind whipped her wet hair across her face, making it difficult to see. Hail pelted her skin, sending sharp stinging pains with each hit.

The slippery grass made it difficult for them to keep their footing, but the overhead trees kept some of the hail at bay. They hurried as fast as they could until they reached the sheltered porch. Chase dug in his pocket, pulled out a set of keys, and quickly unlocked the door.

Once inside, they stood in the foyer, dripping and catching their breath.

"That storm sure came out of nowhere." Camara shuddered before removing her life jacket and Windbreaker.

"I should have been paying more attention." Chase removed his life jacket. He took hers from her, laid them both on a bench in the foyer, and then faced her. "I had my mind on other things." He stepped closer. Camara stepped backward until her back pressed against the wall. Placing his arms on each side of her with his hands flat against the wall, he stared down at her. Rain dripped from his hair, and water beaded on his face and lips. Chase dipped his head toward her. Camara's insides shook, not only from being chilled but from knowing what was about to happen.

His mouth touched hers in a questioning kiss. When she responded, he pulled her into his arms and kissed her thoroughly. How could the man she'd been rivals with for so many years make her go weak in the knees with his toe-tingling kiss? More to the point, how could she be kissing a guy she'd vowed not to trust only half an hour before? Nothing was making sense. Pushing him away was a viable option, but right then, as dumb as it was, she didn't want to.

When he pulled back, Camara looked into his eyes, feeling a bit awkward.

"We'd better get dried off." His drawl was low and shaky. He backed up, putting space between them. After that kiss, she needed plenty of space . . . and air.

"Is that you, Chase?"

Camara spun toward the sound of the deep male voice.

"Hello, Roberts." Chase nudged Camara forward toward the handsome man who appeared to be in his mid-forties. With his dark hair, blue eyes, and medium build, he reminded her of Clark Gable.

"This is my friend, Camara. Camara, this is Mr. Daniel Roberts."

She tried not to stare at him as they shook hands.

"He and his wife live in the cottage out back. They've taken care of this place since I was four."

"Oh." She nodded, not knowing what else to say.

"Nice to meet you, miss."

"Chase!" A beautiful, petite blond woman ran toward them and threw her arms around Chase. "When I saw that storm coming in, I was so worried about you." She stepped back and looked at Camara. The lady's large green eyes sparkled when she looked at her.

"This is my friend, Camara. Camara, this is Mrs. Helen Roberts."

"Pleasure to meet you, ma'am." The lady shook her hand.

Helen stepped back. "You're soaked. We need to get you into some dry clothes." She eyed her up and down. "We're about the same size. I have something that'll fit you."

Camara looked at Chase, who smiled sheepishly at her.

"Follow me." Helen smiled.

Relieved to get rid of her wet clothes, Camara gladly followed the woman.

Chase couldn't help admiring her feminine walk. She was a complete enigma to him. She could repair and build trucks and outdo any man, but she could be feminine and sweet with equal ease. She was the most desirable woman he'd ever met. Whenever he'd teased her lately, he did it because it gave him an excuse to be around her. He might have taken on his dad's attitude toward the Coles for a time, but that was long over. He wanted to pursue a relationship with Camara and see where it would lead.

He couldn't believe he'd kissed her. His heart was still racing. He'd waited for her to shove him away, but when she didn't, he pulled her closer and deepened the kiss. And what a kiss. Who would have thought that feisty little mechanic could kiss with such passion? But, he realized, everything Camara did, she did passionately.

"Reliving that kiss?" Roberts asked, nudging him.

Chase felt heat rise from his stomach to his face, even though Roberts and Helen were more like family to him than his father's employees.

"Don't worry. I won't tell Helen. If I did, she'd have the two of you married off next week." He chuckled. "Thanks for giving us plenty of notice. Helen has everything ready, just as you asked. I hope your guest enjoys her meal. Talk to you later."

Chase nodded. Taking the steps two at a time, he went to his room and changed into some dry clothes. He couldn't wait to see Camara's face. With his dad out of town until Tuesday, Chase confidently arranged a surprise luncheon, regardless of his dad's insistence on being informed whenever anyone used the place. Chase had only himself to blame. On his sixteenth birthday, he'd secretly thrown a wild party and his friends had trashed the house.

He hurried back downstairs, grabbed the fireplace remote, and turned it on. Then he rushed into the kitchen, making sure Helen had everything ready. He wanted today to be special. Plus, he wanted to show Camara that he wasn't the same jerk he had been in the past.

"Chase." He heard Camara calling.

"Be right there," he hollered. Seeing everything was ready, he headed back to the living room.

Camara stood in front of the white marble fireplace with her hands extended toward the flames. The homey image sucked the breath out of him. Wearing a white sweat suit with a towel wrapped around her head, she looked as if she belonged there. That idea did funny things to his insides.

He drew in a breath and cleared his throat. "Lunch is ready," he said, walking up behind her. Chase offered her his arm. When she slipped her hand through his elbow, his stomach quivered. Never before had a woman's touch affected him so strongly. What was it about her that made his body tingle and his heart race ninety miles per hour?

The afternoon flew by in a flurry. After an intimate lunch, the two of them had talked and played games with the Robertses. Even though she understood why Chase wanted to get the boat across the lake before dark, the thought of leaving made Camara sad.

When they stepped outside, the thick humidity dampened her clothes. Orange, yellow, and silver danced throughout the lake's ripples as the sun lowered against the horizon. The trip back was quiet and serene until they neared the marina. Camara heard Chase groan.

"What's wrong?" she asked, sitting forward.

Chase jerked his chin once toward the wharf.

Her stomach plunged to her toes.

Chase expertly guided the pontoon boat against the dock. Before Camara rose, his dad hopped on the boat and glared hard at her.

"Get away from my son!"

Camara blinked at his animosity.

In horror, Chase gasped. "Dad!"

"Stay out of this, Chase." Mr. Lamar pinned her with his gaze. "I warned you to stay away from my son. Now do it or else," he ground out.

Stunned, Camara barely heard the protest Chase aimed at his father. Then as quickly as he'd arrived, he left, leaving in his wake a heavy foreboding feeling. Camara glanced at Chase standing with his mouth agape.

Knowing Chase had to secure the boat before he could leave, Camara snatched up her bag and fled. This time his dad's threats had truly frightened her. For Chase's sake as well as her own, she needed to avoid him.

She ran several minutes before ducking into a bait shop. She stayed close to the bathroom door in case she saw Chase; that way she could slip inside so he wouldn't find her. Once the coast was clear, she'd call a cab.

CHAPTER 11

Chase pulled his Ford behind Camara's Hummer parked in front of the dilapidated house. The shingles were all but gone from the roof, the steps needed repair, three of the windows were boarded, the paint had peeled, and the railing on the porch was missing in several places. The place was devoid of grass. The only color was a variety of bright wild flowers dotting the yard. Pine trees surrounded the house.

Looking for Camara, Chase scanned the volunteer workers from Living Water Fellowship. When he didn't see her, disappointment shrouded him. He was hoping to get a chance to speak to her alone today because she'd avoided him since their date. He wasn't about to let his dad's negative attitude stop him from getting to know Camara. On Pastor Stephans's advice, Chase had confronted his father and let him know that his vendetta against the Coles was just that — his. And Chase would no longer be a part of it. Nor would he let him control his life any longer.

That hadn't gone over well, but he couldn't worry about it right now.

Chase grabbed a can of paint and a brush from the church van. In hopes of finding her, he headed around the back of the house and spotted her standing by herself stripping old paint from a window.

He quietly walked up beside her. "Can we talk?"

Camara held her scraper in midair. She didn't turn. Chase held his breath and wondered if she would bolt.

After what seemed like an eternity, she faced him. She removed her Chevy cap, tucked her hair behind her ears, and looked him in the eye. "Look, I don't want your dad seeing us together." She put her cap back on her head.

"My dad isn't gonna come clear out here. Besides —"

"The point isn't whether or not your dad will come out here, Chase." She set the scraper on the windowsill. "Your dad hates me." She closed her eyes briefly, picked up the scraper, and started removing the peeled paint again.

Chase grabbed her free hand. "Listen to

me, Camara." He turned her face toward his. "I don't care what my dad thinks. I'm a grown man. His problems with your family are just that — *his* problems. Not mine." He searched her eyes. "I care about you, and I want to see where this relationship will go."

"There can be no relationship. Don't you see that?" Her big brown eyes looked sad. Or maybe it was just wishful thinking on his part that she was as bothered about the situation as he was. "Your dad will make both of our lives miserable."

"I won't let him, Camara. I'm not afraid of —"

Camara cut him off. "I don't want a rift coming between you and your father because of me. Family is too important."

Her concern for him touched Chase deeply. It proved she did care.

"Ah, Cammy." He pulled her into his arms. She tried to push away from him, but he held her tighter and whispered against her ear. "I appreciate your considering how our relationship will affect me and my dad's, but . . ." He released her enough to look into her eyes. "I told my father I loved him, but I refused to be a part of his grudge against your family." He gazed intently at her. "And that I wasn't going to stop seeing you, either."

Chase felt her tense. When she backed out of his arms, he didn't stop her. After sharing his heart, he wanted her to be in his arms because she wanted to be, not because he forced her to.

She looked up at him. "What did he say?"

"It doesn't matter what he said, Camara. I won't have my dad controlling and manipulating my life anymore. He's done that my whole life, and I'm tired of it." He cupped her chin. "And I don't want you avoiding me, Cam. I had a great time the other day, and I'd like to spend more time with you." Uncertainty danced in her eyes. If only there was something he could say to reassure her. "How about if after church on Sunday, we go to Swamper's together and watch Erik run his monster truck?"

She didn't answer him. Instead she turned and started scraping the old paint chips off the windowsill.

Happy voices rose above the noise of the electric saws. Symphonic hammering echoed through the woods. Several buzzing bees landed on nearby azalea blooms. And yet the silence was killing him.

"Will your dad be there?" she asked softly without looking at him.

"Nope. He's leaving Saturday evening

145

after the mud bog races and won't be back till Monday night."

She scraped more paint off then looked at him. "Okay." She smiled shyly. "I'd like that. But" — she tilted her head sideways — "I'll ride with Erik and meet you there."

"That'll work." Chase held up the can of paint he had in his hand. "I guess I'd better get busy."

His heart felt light and carefree again. But as soon as he thought about his dad's threats, uneasiness settled over him. He wasn't sure if his dad would follow through with them or not. As much as Chase didn't want to fight with his dad, he refused to let his father's unforgiveness ruin his chance at a happy future. And Chase had a feeling his happy future included Camara.

Removing the straps from The Black Beast, Camara kept glancing toward the entrance into Swamper Speedway. The thought of seeing Chase sent a fluttering feeling through her. How would her nervous stomach survive until their date tomorrow evening?

She still couldn't believe that she, Camara Cole, had gone out with Chase Lamar. What had equally surprised her was she'd had an amazing time, and his kiss had weakened her knees. Who would have thought Chase Lamar could kiss like that? He certainly wasn't the same awful person she'd known all those years. This new Chase seemed to be a sweetheart.

She struggled to get the latch loose on a strap. Too bad Erik wasn't here today. But there was a problem at Daddy's dealership, and Erik had to take care of it. Tugging at the latch with all her might, Camara finally got it unsnapped.

At the familiar sound of Chase's Ford diesel, Camara's heart sped up and matched the timing of his truck engine. *Crr crr crr crr . . . thump thump thump thump.* In between the row of rich green dogwood trees she spotted it. Not wanting to get caught looking for him, she quickly dropped the ramps, climbed into her bog truck, fired it up, and put it in reverse. Making sure her tires lined up on the ramps, she eased her truck off the trailer. She pulled The Black Beast next to her trailer and shut it off.

From the corner of her eye, she watched to see where Chase parked. Her stomach dipped. Chase parked close to the registration stand on the opposite end of the contestants' pit from her. She wondered why until she noticed his dad climbing out of the passenger's side.

Camara grabbed her stepladder, popped the hood of her truck, and started her usual routine, checking everything out.

"Hey, beautiful."

Camara jerked upward, banging her head on the hood.

"Ouch. Bet that hurt. You all right?" Chase asked.

She hopped down and rubbed the back of her head. "I'm fine."

"I thought I'd come over and say hi before both of us got too busy." Chase looked at the truck with its hood raised. "Is something wrong?"

"Nope, just making sure everything's running okay."

"It's a Chevy. How can it be okay?" His dark green eyes twinkled with mirth.

Camara tilted her head and scrunched her face.

Chase held up his hands. "Sorry, I couldn't resist."

"Well, it's better than a For—" Camara's jibe stopped on her lips when she noticed Mr. Lamar glaring their way.

Chase followed her gaze. "Don't pay any attention to him. It's his problem, not ours."

His dad yanked on the nylon straps holding the Mud Boss. "I'd better go before Dad breaks a strap." His look was apologetic.

Camara fought back her disappointment. "Yeah, probably so. Talk to ya later." She gathered her tools and put them in her yellow toolbox.

She watched Chase and his dad leave the Mud Boss and stand in a long line at a faraway concession stand. With only a handful of people in the contestants' pit this early in the morning, Camara realized this was her chance to leave her truck unattended and go register. Knowing she'd be back in a flash, she sprinted toward the registration booth.

By the time she reached the line, four people had gotten in ahead of her. Anxious and nervous about not being able to see The Black Beast from where she stood, Camara shifted her weight back and forth. If only this blasted entry booth didn't obstruct her view, then she could relax. When her turn came, Camara quickly grabbed the clipboard and furiously filled out the forms then handed them to Sam. When she stepped around the corner, she saw Chase standing by The Black Beast, looking around.

"Camara!" Sam hollered.

"Yeah." She ducked her head back around the corner of the booth.

"You forgot to give me your entry fee."

Ack! Camara jerked it out of her pocket and handed it to him. By the time she got to the end of the booth again, Chase and his dad were nowhere to be seen. She scanned the area again just to make sure. When she couldn't find them, a mixture of relief and anxiety filled her stomach. At least she could avoid another horrible encounter with Mr. Lamar when she passed the Mud Boss on the way back to her truck. Now, if she could only calm her nervous stomach. But that wasn't likely to happen anytime soon. She couldn't stop her thoughts from wondering where Chase and his dad were and what they'd been up to.

Camara picked up speed as she walked past Chase's rig.

Mr. Lamar stepped out in front of her.

Camara stopped abruptly, barely missing plowing into him.

"What part of 'Stay away from my son' don't you understand?" Mr. Lamar's nostrils flared, and his eyes narrowed into tiny slits.

Fear raced through Camara.

"What's going on here?" Chase's voice boomed from beside her, causing her to jump.

Wide-eyed, Camara spun her gaze toward Chase, then his dad. The hatred in Mr.

Lamar's eyes as he glared at her made her insides rattle like a loose muffler. Not wanting to be in the middle of this war, Camara whirled and sprinted toward her bogger.

"Why can't you accept the fact I like her, Dad? I told you, this is your battle with them. Not mine. I love you. But I'm a grown man. I'm not a child anymore."

His dad snorted derisively. "A grown man who lives off his father's money."

Chase's stomach plummeted. Even though he oversaw one of his dad's Ford dealerships and earned every penny he got, his dad didn't see it that way. As far as he was concerned, it was still Lamar money.

Chase gathered his courage. "I work hard for what you pay me."

"It's still *my* money." His dad stepped closer. "I'm telling you, if you don't quit associating with them people, then you leave me no choice but to fire you and withdraw you from my will. I will not have disloyal employees."

The look of triumph on his father's face sickened Chase. Is that what he was to his dad? An employee? In that instant, Chase decided he would no longer tolerate his dad's controlling personality.

"You won't have to fire me. I quit." In five

long strides, Chase hopped in his Coupe.

"Those Coles will pay for stealing my son. I'll personally see to it," Chase heard his dad growl before he stomped in the other direction.

Chase placed his palms against the steering wheel and laid his forehead against his knuckles. "God, protect the Coles from my father. He's so full of bitterness and unforgiveness toward them it's making him act like a lunatic." Chase thought about his dad disinheriting him. If he did, Chase would have to deal with it. He could no longer handle his dad's hatefulness. Chase raised his head and swiped the moistness from his eyes. He fired up the Mud Boss and headed toward the lineup. It was his turn to race.

Trying to draw comfort from the fact that he had made some sound investments and could live quite comfortably without his job, Chase worked through the details of that. But the idea of his dad disowning him broke his heart. Chase might not like what his father was doing, but he still loved him.

Father, give me the grace and the wisdom I need to handle this whole situation.

He lined up at the pits, and in spite of being upset, he still made a great run. When he got back to his rig, his dad was nowhere around. Wondering how his dad got home,

Chase looked around and noticed that Bobby-Rae's vehicle was no longer parked next to him. Chase found that strange, considering Bobby-Rae never left until the races were over. He thought about how his dad and Bobby-Rae had gotten awful chummy lately — which was odd since the man worked for the Coles. But then again, everything his dad did lately surprised him.

Stan and Tim lined up in front of the pits. Camara was up after them. Her dad and brothers had arrived moments before, after resolving the crisis at the dealership, and Erik held the door open for her. She jumped in and fired up The Black Beast. It missed and shook like an out-of-balance tire. She jammed the emergency brake and jumped out. Popping the hood, she quickly grabbed her stepladder and checked the distributor cap. The screws were loose. Someone had tampered with her truck . . . again. If only she hadn't been so upset earlier by Mr. Lamar's tirade, then she would have thought to recheck The Black Beast after she'd left it unattended. Desperately she wanted to share her encounter with someone, but what good would it do? The only One who could do anything about it was God. *Lord* —

"What's wrong, sis?" Erik asked from

behind her.

Lots, she wanted to say. But instead she chose to pray about it later. Right now she needed to deal with her truck. "Someone loosened the distributor cap." She jiggled the cap.

"How do you know someone messed with it?"

"Because I made sure it was tight this morning when I got here." She stuck her head out from under the hood. "Will you grab my toolbox from off the floorboard?"

Erik nodded. Camara ducked back under the hood. In seconds he was back. He handed her the distributor wrench. Adrenaline running at full speed, Camara adjusted the distributor until the engine ran smoothly again. After tightening the distributor in place, she grabbed her tools and hopped down.

"Thanks, bubba. I gotta hurry." She slammed the hood and hustled into the cab.

After tugging on her helmet, she pulled on her harness and clamped it; then she slid her hands into her leather gloves. Making sure the coast was clear, she backed out of her spot and rumbled her way toward the pit. Camara drew in a long breath and exhaled slowly, trying to gear down her anger. Whoever did this to her would not get the best of her. She had to get out there and win.

She rolled her window down so she could hang her head out if need be. Her mission — to flash in and out of that pit like lightning. And no mud-covered windshield, no poor sportsmanship, no male chauvinist, or no anything would stop her from accomplishing that feat.

With her eye on the flagman, she inched The Black Beast forward until he clenched his fist, her signal to stop.

She riveted her gaze on the flagman.

He raised the flag.

With shaky hands, Camara flipped the master switch, engaging the nitrous. She held the brake and pressed the gas.

The flag dropped.

Camara jerked her foot off the brake and shoved the gas pedal to the floor. She lunged into the pit ahead of Tom Combs's Ford Bronco, the Aggressive Digger.

Her Chevy flew so fast through the mud pit it felt like The Black Beast was on top of it instead of in it.

Her heart revved as fast as her truck. She lunged up and out of the pit and didn't bother looking back. Instead of heading straight toward the contestants' pit, Camara pulled off to the side, jerked off her helmet and harness, and listened for her time.

The announcer's voice echoed over the loudspeaker. "Well, how about that, folks! We have a new record here today. Camara Cole's time is 8.48!" Camara's mouth fell open. "Let's give her a big round of applause."

Camara pumped her arm in the air. "Yes! Yes! Yes!"

Her truck jerked forward as she headed back toward the pit as fast as safety would allow. The second she put it in park and shut the engine off, the door flew open. Erik jerked her out and swung her around. "Way to go, Cam!"

When her feet touched the ground, Tony and Daddy took turns hugging her and congratulating her. None of them seemed to mind the mud draped over her because Slick grabbed her and lifted her off her feet, as well.

"Guess you showed them, huh, sis," Slick said proudly while setting her down. He glanced at her bog truck. "You're gonna have fun getting all that mud out of the inside of the cab. That'll teach ya to leave the window down." He tapped her chin with his forefinger and stepped back to let other well-wishers in.

Several minutes later when the congratulations died down, Camara set about hosing off The Black Beast. Whoever had messed with her truck must feel sick that their plan didn't work. She wondered who could possibly hate her so much that they would do such a cruel thing. Instantly Mr. Lamar's venomous eyes sparked through her mind. Was he the one sabotaging her truck? She searched her memory in hopes of finding the answer to that question. Suddenly she realized Mr. Lamar wasn't around her truck every time it had been messed with. But Chase was. A nauseous feeling hit her stomach. Everything inside her desperately wanted to believe it wasn't . . .

She envisioned Chase at church — tears flowing down his cheeks. *Oh, God, I'm so confused. I don't know what to think. Did Chase do it, or didn't he? Can I trust him?* The longer she mulled it over, the more convinced she was that Chase had loosened the distributor cap. After all, he'd done the same thing in the past, along with loosening a nut here and a spark plug wire there. And he *was* the only person she'd seen around her truck today. Camara groaned. If only she would have waited until Lolly or one of her family members had arrived before registering, then none of this would have happened. What an idiot she'd been for leaving her truck unattended and allowing herself to get suckered in by Chase's good looks and charm. Camara wanted to slap herself for trusting him. Well, never again.

"Is that what you meant, Dad?" Chase moved his cell phone to the opposite ear. "Did you do something to Camara's truck?" Chase fought the urge to run over and congratulate Camara. Instead he had to find out if his father was behind her truck running so poorly. After all, he did say he'd make the Coles pay. And what better way than to mess with Camara's truck and keep her from winning?

"What do you mean?" His dad's voice sounded phony.

Chase removed his hat, wiped the sweat off his forehead, and replaced his cap. The hot sun grilled him, and the humidity clung to his body, making him drip with sweat. "You know what I mean, Dad. Camara's truck wasn't running right."

"Did she have trouble?" Chase knew his dad's concern wasn't real.

"Yeah, she had trouble."

"Oh, that's too bad."

"Well, it doesn't matter now." Chase paused, waiting to see if his dad would ask him why. When he didn't, Chase continued.

158

"Camara broke the track record."

"She *what?*" The question was more of a shriek. "How can that be?"

"How can what be, Dad?" Chase asked innocently. He just knew his dad had done something. He wanted to let him know his plan didn't work.

"Nothing. You just said that something was wrong with it, and now she's gone and broke the track record. Your record." The hate inside his father came through loud and clear.

"She got it fixed before she ran. Guess whoever did it feels pretty rotten about now. It only made her more determined than ever to win. So their plan backfired."

"What makes you think someone did this? As far as I can see, she's just a lousy mechanic."

Chase shook his head and glanced heavenward. "She's not a lousy mechanic, Dad. She's one of Alabama's best."

"I don't have time for this," his dad barked and hung up on him.

With a click, he shut off his cell phone and headed toward Camara. He couldn't wait to congratulate her.

"Hey, beautiful. Congratulations on —"

"Don't you ever come near me again, Chase Lamar!" Camara snapped then turned the sprayer off.

Stunned, Chase stopped in his tracks and stared at her. "What's wrong?" He stepped closer and laid his hand on hers. She jerked her arm away.

"As if you don't know," she ground out. "Did you really think I was that stupid?" Her big brown eyes shot flaming arrows his way. "You thought you could befriend me, get me to like you, and even take me out on a date so you could win my trust. I should have known better than to trust you. Well, your plan didn't work, did it?" The smug look on her face felt like a slap to his.

"What plan are you ranting about?"

Camara spun the bill of her Chevy cap around.

Oops. Wrong choice of words. That meant only one thing: She was madder than an angry bull.

"As if you don't know," she bit out. "Stay away from my truck and from me."

"Camara?" Chase grabbed her hands. She tried getting free from his grasp, but Chase clutched her tighter. His stomach lodged in his throat.

"Leave me alone!" She squirmed.

"What's going on here?" Erik asked, looking at Camara then at Chase.

Chase dropped her hands. "That's what

160

I'd like to know."

"Chase sabotaged my truck. That's what's going on."

Chase's eyes widened along with Erik's. "What?" Chase blurted. "You think *I* messed with your truck?"

"Cam, you don't mean that," Erik said incredulously.

"Oh yes, I do. I checked everything out when I got here today." She glared at Chase.

"What's that got to do with anything?" her brother asked.

Camara faced Erik and planted her hands on her hips. "You're taking *his* side?"

"No. I'm just trying to get to the bottom of this thing."

"Well, look no further, bubba." She pointed at Chase. "He did it." The disdainful look she sent Chase made him inwardly cringe. He still wasn't over the shock of her thinking he'd messed with her truck. "When I was busy registering, he" — she jerked her thumb Chase's way — "loosened the distributor cap."

"What makes you think that?"

Chase wanted to hear the answer to Erik's question, too.

"Because I saw *him*" — Camara pointed toward Chase — "hanging around my truck. He knows I'm his biggest competition, and he can't stand the thought of me, a mere female, beating him."

Chase couldn't believe what he was hearing. He may have stooped that low in the past, but didn't she believe he'd changed now? From the accusing look on her face, she didn't. *Lord, show me what to do.*

"Listen, Cammy," Chase said.

"Don't call me that. It's *Camara* to you," she snapped.

"Camara." He paused and gathered his composure. "I'd hoped by now you would have noticed Christ has changed me." He searched her eyes looking for any sign she believed him. He saw a spark of softness, so he continued. "I know I used to sabotage your truck just to win. But please believe me when I say I'm not now. I promise you, I will find out who is, though." He nodded toward Erik then looked back at Camara. "Good luck on your next run. And congratulations for breaking the track record. I'm proud of you." With that, he turned and headed toward his Coupe.

As he walked, he shook his head slowly. *Lord, show me if my father really is behind this. If not him, then please help me find out who is.* A knot lodged in his gut. It broke his heart to think Camara thought he'd messed with her truck. The old Chase might have allowed her to believe it was him and even found pleasure in it. But now that he loved her, he couldn't stand the thought of her not liking him or thinking badly of him. Chase stopped and removed his cap. The realization that he loved her yanked the air from his lungs. He ran his hand over his short hair and replaced his cap. Until he proved his innocence, he knew Camara wouldn't have anything to do with him. Well, he would find out who the culprit was. And whoever it was would pay. He'd see to it personally.

"Camara, how many times do I have to tell you your stubborn pride is going to ruin you?" Camara's father's voice came from behind her.

Camara spun around. "What do you mean?"

"I heard you accuse Chase of messing with your truck. When are you going to get it through your head that Chase has changed since giving his life to Christ?"

"But, Daddy . . ." Camara set her socket wrench down. "He was the only one hanging around my truck, looking all suspicious-like. And someone *did* mess with it." She looked at the ground and kicked some gravel with her toe. "What if he's just using me to gain my trust?"

Her father's brows rose. "You don't really believe that, do you?"

She shrugged.

"Camara, sweetheart. You need to be careful accusing people. 'Judge not, that you be not judged. For with what judgment you judge, you will be judged; and with the measure you use, it will be measured back to you.'" Her father's eyes held only compassion. "You need to pray and ask God to reveal the truth to you." He laid his hand on her shoulder and squeezed. "In the meantime, you owe that man an apology."

"But I don't know that he *didn't* do it."

"That may be true. But you don't know that he did, either." He grew quiet for a minute. Camara knew he was thinking. "What if the situation were reversed and Chase had accused you?"

"Me?" she squeaked. "I wouldn't stoop that low. Besides, my Chevy could beat his Ford any day."

"Baby girl." He pushed himself off her vehicle and stood to his full six foot two inches. "You have judged, convicted, and sentenced that poor man without any proof. Do you really want that judgment to come back on you? And what kind of mercy would you want in a case like this?"

Although Camara felt Chase might still be guilty, she knew she had sinned against the Lord by judging him too quickly.

"Listen to me." He clutched her face in his large hands. "Don't let your pride cost you the love of a good man."

Love of a good man? Chase didn't love her. And she definitely didn't love him.

Camara needed time to think. She glanced at her watch. It would be an hour before her second run. "I'll be back." She hugged him. "Thanks, Daddy." She headed toward the thicket of dogwood trees behind the speedway.

"Chase?"

Chase wiggled himself out from under his Coupe. Camara stood over him, tucking her hair nervously behind her ears and looking at the ground.

He stood and dusted the dirt off his shirt. "Hi." He suddenly felt shy and uncertain about what to say. Deciding to let her do the talking, he just watched her.

"Look, I'm sorry for accusing you of sabotaging my truck. It was wrong, and I apologize." She looked up at him.

"What made you realize I didn't do it?"

Camara frowned. "Nothing. I'm still not sure that you did or didn't."

Chase felt like he'd been sucker punched. She still believed he was guilty.

"I just wanted to let you know that I accused you without having proof. My father showed me how wrong I was to do that."

"Cam, thank you for apologizing. But I had nothing to do with messing up your truck."

Chase reached for her hands, but she jerked them behind her back. "Daddy always says that the truth has a way of speaking. And until I find out the truth, I'm canceling our date." She looked him square in the eye. "I won't be made a fool of." She whirled and sprinted off.

Chase fought to breathe. *God, You've got to help me find out who did this. I don't wanna lose her.*

CHAPTER 12

Chase missed Camara. When she hadn't shown up for church the next day, the word *disappointment* hardly did justice to the feeling. And he hadn't seen or heard from her all week. He stared out his office window at the mechanic shop below. Someday, Lord willing, he'd own his auto shop. He arched his back to get the kinks out. Two and a half hours of paperwork and he was caught up. He glanced at the clock: 6:45 a.m. Time to go. He made a quick phone call to John, telling him he'd be by in a few minutes to pick him up.

He couldn't wait to get to Swamper's and see Camara. There was no way she'd miss a mud bog race. Especially now that the two of them were tied in points.

In some ways he wanted Camara to win, but his old fleshly nature, the competitor side of him, hadn't been crucified yet. He'd even thought about switching from nitrous to alcohol. But knowing how hard it was on engines, he decided not to. He'd just have to leave the race results in God's hands. If it was God's will that Camara won, so be it.

He pulled into Swamper's and looked for Camara's rig. Disappointment draped over him. This was the first time he had arrived before Camara. She had remained true to her word by keeping her distance from him. *Lord, please show me what to do to make things right with her. Expose whoever is doing this.*

He turned to John. "Don't forget, John. We have to keep an eye on Camara's vehicle. While I'm running, you watch it close, okay?" He parked his rig.

"Gotcha, boss."

"And stop with the boss thing already. We're friends first." John had been Chase's employee for four years now. No matter how mean Chase had been to him and no matter how much he'd made fun of John's God, John had never retaliated. Instead he always had a peace about him that Chase envied. One day he had vowed to find out what John had that he didn't.

Chase's life had never been the same since then. In fact, it was because of John that he could face his job every day. And after his father had paid him a surprise visit last

Saturday night asking Chase if he would reconsider working for him again, Chase had wanted to honor his father, so he went back. If he could be half the light to his dad that John was to him, he would be happy.

They got out of Chase's pickup and removed the straps on the Coupe.

Chase hopped in the Coupe, drove it off the trailer, and parked it.

The sound of tires crunching on gravel grabbed Chase's attention. His heart skipped a beat. Camara's Hummer and Erik's semi rounded the corner. Chase had parked close to where Camara normally parked. The closer she got, the faster his heart beat. However, when she drove right by him without even looking his way and parked clear down on the far end, he groaned.

John laid his hand on Chase's arm. "Trust God, Chase. He's the only One who can take care of this whole mess."

Chase forced his eyes away from Camara and onto John. "Thanks, John. Keep praying, will ya?"

"I haven't stopped since you told me what happened." John smiled.

Chase had never had a friend he trusted enough to confide in until John. After watching his integrity for years, Chase knew

John was a man to be trusted.

Erik headed toward him. He was another person Chase knew he could trust.

"Good morning." Erik shook John's hand and then Chase's. "I want you to know that no matter what happens between you and my sister, you'll always be my friend." Erik glanced toward Camara, then back at Chase. "Don't let it get to ya." Erik squeezed his shoulder. "She'll come around. And for what it's worth, I know you didn't mess with her truck."

Bobby-Rae pulled up alongside them in his Chevy and said something. Chase couldn't make out his words because of his loud exhaust.

"Excuse me." Chase walked around to the driver's side. "I didn't hear that. What'd ya say?"

"I said . . . good luck today." Bobby-Rae looked around and lowered his voice. "I'm sure glad you installed NOS. Us guys have to show Camara how it's done." He gave a derisive snort and drove off. Chase stood there, frowning. How did Bobby-Rae know he'd installed NOS? The only ones who knew were Erik, Camara, John, and his dad.

"What'd he want?" Erik asked from beside Chase.

Chase repeated what Bobby-Rae had said.

"He's been downright belligerent to Camara lately."

"Why?" John asked.

Good question, Chase thought. And he planned on finding out the answer.

Camara was up next. For her second run, she was side by side with Chase. Even though she had forgiven him, she still didn't trust him. Trust was something you learned as a child and earned as an adult. He hadn't earned hers yet. And she wasn't certain he ever would.

Chase revved his engine. Camara refused to look at him. Instead she focused on the flagman. Her heart thumped wildly against her ribs, and her trembling body matched the vibration of her bog truck.

The flag rose.

Camara flipped the master switch, pressed the brake, and then the gas pedal. The engine roared. The exhaust rumbled.

The flag dropped.

Camara jerked her foot off the brake, shoved the gas pedal to the floor, and drove like a woman on a mission through the pit. She did a quick glance sideways. Chase was nowhere in view. She lunged up and out of the pit. Without a backward glance, Camara headed toward the contestants' area.

Erik jerked open her door. "Wow. What-ever you were trying to prove certainly worked."

"Good," she said with no emotion.

Shutting off The Black Beast, she removed her helmet, gloves, and harness and jumped out. Before her first run, someone had let the air out of both tires on the passenger side. Thank the good Lord she'd had a compressor. As much as she hated where her thoughts were taking her, she couldn't shake the feeling that Chase was somehow behind it. It couldn't have been Mr. Lamar. He wasn't even at the track today. Daddy said not to judge, but all the evidence was stacked against Chase. It broke her heart because she'd really had a good time with him. But Camara knew from experience that even so-called Christians hurt and used other people to get what they wanted. And besides, she really didn't know Chase all that well.

Absentmindedly, Camara dug the mud out of the tire grooves. The announcer's voice came over the loudspeaker. "Camara's on a roll today, folks. Her time is 8.9. Chase Lamar's time is 9.22." Camara heard what she'd wanted to hear. But she was too numb to enjoy it.

"Congratulations, Camara." Chase's voice

sounded from behind her.

She turned and faced him. "Thanks," she said glumly. She turned and walked to the front of her pickup. From the corner of her eye, she watched him leave. It ripped the air from her lungs.

"Don't let it go to your head. It won't happen again."

Camara whirled to find Bobby-Rae glaring at her. "What's your problem, Bobby-Rae? You jealous?"

"Of you?" he scoffed. "Not hardly."

"Well, I don't see you winning."

"That's cuz I don't have a rich daddy giving me everything I want."

"Neither do I. I work hard for my money."

"Yeah, right." Bobby-Rae snickered snidely.

Camara turned her cap around.

"Just you wait. By the end of this season, I'll have enough money to build a better bogger and to afford NOS, too." He jerked his head forward and snorted. "It'll make yours look like a puddle jumper."

"We'll see."

"Yeah, we will."

Having had enough of him, Camara shoved her way past him, started the pressure washer, and began hosing off The Black Beast.

What was his problem anyway? Was he still angry with her for turning him down? She huffed out a breath. If his lousy attitude continued, she'd talk to Erik about transferring him to a different shop. For months now, the guy had treated her like dirt. She had enough stress in her life without having to put up with the likes of him.

Camara's gaze drifted toward Chase's rig. Her biggest stress came not from her desire to win but from her dilemma where Chase was concerned. She really liked him, but as hard as she tried to believe in him and trust him, she just couldn't. The thought of never spending another day with Chase like she had at his family's lake house caused a wave of sadness to gush over her. She sucked in big gulps of air. She had to get away from here — and fast.

CHAPTER 13

Camara couldn't believe it was Friday, the Fourth of July, already. Where had the time gone? She'd had so much to do at work that the week had flown by.

After filling all her bird feeders with birdseed, she walked to her patio and sat on a lounge chair. She closed her eyes, tilted her face toward the morning sun, and soaked up the warmth spreading across her face. A symphony of birds caused her body to relax.

She drew in a deep breath. For a month now there had been no more incidents with The Black Beast. Whoever had been sabotaging her truck must have finally given up. Or they realized they had no chance of messing with it since someone stayed near it all the time.

Once again, she and Chase were tied in points. Since he had installed NOS, one week she'd win and the next he did. It saddened her a bit to think there were only six more races till the end of the racing season.

Camara picked up her coffee, took a long drink, and enjoyed the warm liquid as it slid down her throat. Then she picked up her Bible and let it fall open. As she flipped through the pages, several scriptures about forgiveness and pride seemed to leap off the pages, convicting her about her attitude. Flipping the pages again, her gaze landed on a scripture about the accuser of our brethren. She thought about how she'd been accusing Chase and wondered if Satan had used her to falsely accuse him.

"Camara."

At the sound of Chase's voice, Camara jumped and nearly sent her Bible toppling. She caught it before it slid off her lap. She swung her legs off her lounge chair and planted her feet on the cool concrete.

"What are you doing here?" She wanted to be angry at him for showing up unannounced, but noting the look of uncertainty on his face, she couldn't. In spite of what she believed he'd done to her truck, she had missed him.

"I know it's only eight thirty, and I'm sorry to barge in on you like this, but I was hoping you were up and about."

"Why?"

"Well, I wondered if we could talk." His eyes held such hope that she found she couldn't refuse him.

"Okay." She laid her Bible on a patio end table and motioned to an empty chair across from her, as a soft breeze rustled the azalea bushes in her yard. "Please have a seat."

Chase took the seat across from her. Camara held her breath in anticipation of what he had to say.

"Listen. I want you to know I talked to Stan last night, and he told me how Lolly saw me near your truck again the day you had the flat tires. I was, but I didn't mess with it." She looked for any kind of deception in his eyes but saw none. "I was waiting for you. You can ask John. He was there with me."

Camara didn't know what to think. She rose, put her back to him, and crossed her arms. Had she misjudged him, or were these more mind games?

Chase placed his warm hands on her shoulders. "Cam. I know you think I wanna win at any cost, and the old me would have, but now I would never . . . I repeat, *never* mess with your truck. Please believe me. You can even ask the Lord to show you the truth." His breath felt warm against her ear, sending her body into a shiver spasm.

"You cold?"

Unable to speak past the lump in her throat, she shook her head.

Chase turned her until she faced him. Camara refused to look at him. Instead she focused on a dead bug lying on the concrete patio.

He tilted her chin up. "Please, look at me."

Camara raised her eyes.

"I want you to see the truth in my eyes when I tell you that I did not sabotage your truck. I care too much for you to do something that despicable."

The soft sincerity in Chase's green eyes made her realize that he was telling her the truth. She closed her eyes and released a sigh.

"I'm sorry, Chase. I really don't know what to think anymore." She tucked her hair behind her ears. She owed it to him to be honest. "I'm not used to this new Chase. The old Chase would have done anything to win."

Pain etched his features. "When are you gonna realize that I'm a new creature in Christ? That 'old things have passed away; behold, all things have become new'? Jesus is changing me." He released her chin and turned away from her. "Do you have to keep reminding me of my past mistakes and sins?"

Camara's heart sank. Who was she to hold the past against him? She herself was still dealing with pride. She laid her hand on his arm. His muscle twitched under her palm.

"I'm sorry, Chase. Forgive me." He looked at her with sad eyes. "Please be patient with me. I'm having a hard time getting used to the new you." She tried lightening the mood with a bright smile.

"So is my dad." His voice sounded wistful.

"Your dad?" She tilted her head.

"Forget I said that. How about a truce?" He flashed her a 100-watt smile.

"A truce?" She pinched her lips shut and placed her finger over them. "Hmm. I don't know. That sounds pretty boring."

Chase's brows rose. "Boring?" He dipped his head sideways.

"Yeah. If we call a truce between us, then I won't be able to remind ya how that Ford of yours is full of cobwebs. You know . . . gutless," she said, winking, unable to resist teasing him.

"Hey, all's fair in love and war. At Swamper's, it's war." He pulled her into his arms and captured her gaze. "Here, it's love."

Love? Staring up at him wide-eyed, she watched his face lower, and his lips softly touched hers for a brief moment. Chase's words replayed in Camara's mind. Surely he didn't mean he loved her. And surely he was just using that old cliché. Wasn't he? She wasn't so sure she wanted to find out.

No doubt about it, Chase was in love with Camara. Now all he had to do was win her love. He studied Camara, who still hadn't uttered a word. With dreamy eyes, Miss Tough-As-Nails looked softer than he'd ever seen her before.

Chase cleared his throat. Camara blinked and looked at him. Her face turned pink. Seeing her discomfort, Chase decided to rescue her. "Have you eaten yet? I'm starving. How about we go get some breakfast?"

Camara's stomach chose that moment to growl. She giggled. Her sweet laughter sounded like chimes floating on a gentle breeze.

"You're on. I'll go change."

Chase opened her sliding glass door and allowed her to pass. He slid the door closed and clicked the lock.

Camara raced up the stairs, quickly changed, then slid sidesaddle down the banister. "I'm ready," she announced when her feet hit the floor.

Chase chuckled. "Do you always come down the stairs like that?"

"Only when I'm in a hurry."

With a smile on his face, he headed out the door, and they strolled to his vehicle.

Camara laid her hand on the passenger side door handle.

"Oh no, you don't."

She looked up, surprised. He grabbed her hand and led her to the driver's side and opened it. "I want you sitting next to me." He smiled before placing his hands around her small waist and lifting her up. She weighed no more than a kitten.

She slid over, and he hopped in. Chase placed his arm around her and tucked her tight against his side.

"Chase."

He moved his arm from around her and started the truck. After checking for traffic, he headed down the street. "Yeah?"

"Thanks for coming today and setting things straight."

He glanced at her and noted her shyness.

"I've really missed you," she added softly.

Chase glanced at her. "I've missed you, too." He looked back at the road. Hesitating a moment, he continued. "I don't want anything like this happening again. If we're gonna have any kind of a relationship, we're gonna have to learn to trust each other."

Sitting next to Chase, Camara pondered his words. Did she want a relationship with him? The idea was both frightening and appealing.

"Where are we going anyway?"

"You'll see." He glanced at her. "You don't have any plans for today, do you?" He looked back at the road.

"Only this evening."

"Oh."

Was that disappointment she heard in his voice? "Why?"

"Well, I was wondering if you'd like to spend the day with me."

"Only if you take me to Swamper Speedway this evening. Erik's running his monster truck in a freestyle event tonight. Then they're gonna have a fireworks display afterward."

"Sounds great."

"I should warn you, though. My whole family will be there."

"You mean I don't get you all to myself?" He winked.

"Nope. Take it or leave it."

"I'll take it."

■ ■ ■ ■

The all-day Fourth of July festivities were well on their way at Civitan Park. Many people greeted them as they scanned the concession stands. Once they got their bacon, eggs, grits, and orange juice, they headed toward the covered picnic area.

Stone and cement pillars holding the suspended A-frame roof provided some relief from the sweltering sun. Chase scanned the shelter for an empty picnic table.

"Excuse me." A bald-headed gentleman snagged Chase's attention. "If y'all are lookin' for a place to sit, there's an empty picnic table over there." He pointed to one under a canopy of tall trees.

"Thank you, sir." Chase smiled. "That was right nice of ya."

The man smiled and turned back to his food.

"Man, it's hot, and it's not even nine thirty yet. Today will be another scorcher." Arriving at the table, Chase set their plates down and then sat down across from her so he could see her beautiful face.

He hadn't taken two bites when suddenly someone covered his eyes. "Guess who?"

Chase's heart sank at the sickeningly sweet tone of Brittany van Buran's voice. When would she get the hint that things were over between them? "Brittany," he said none too happily.

"Hi, sweetie. Miss me?" she purred. Wrapping her hands around his neck, she planted a kiss on his mouth.

He pulled her arms from around him and moved her away from him. Chase glanced at Camara, who stared at him wide-eyed. She looked back and forth between him and Brittany. Her brows rose questioningly.

"Now, Chase, sweetie." Brittany ran her hand down his cheek and over his chin. "Is that any way to treat your future wife?"

Chapter 14

The words hit like a punch. Camara slung her legs around the bench, leaped up, and darted off. Once again, he'd made a fool of her. Once again, she'd trusted him and he had smashed her heart to smithereens. How many times would she buy into his lies, fall for his charm, put herself on the chopping block?

"Camara, wait!" She ignored Chase and ran as fast as her short legs would carry her. Not bothering to look back, she headed in the opposite direction of where Chase had parked and lost herself in the throng of people. Making sure she was out of sight, she leaned against a large maple tree. She clutched her aching sides as she gasped to pull air into her starving lungs. The humidity wasn't helping, and neither was the heat. Even the sweet smell of gardenias was enough to turn her stomach.

What was all that garbage about a relationship and trust? How could she have been so stupid? He had a fiancée, for pity's sake. Boy, did he play her for a fool. She swiped at the unwanted tears. Tears over someone she should never have trusted in the first place.

"Camara."

She hunched her shoulders toward the tree, not wanting Chase to see her crying. "Go back to your fiancée."

"Fiancée?" He tried to turn her around, but she brushed his hands off and kept her back to him. "Brittany isn't my fiancée."

Camara blinked away more tears and sniffed. "She asked if that was any way for you to treat your future wife, and she kissed you."

"Ah, Cammy." He laid his hands on her shoulders. "I only dated Brittany for a few weeks last summer. My father wanted us to marry. But he only cared about her father's position as mayor and how good it would make him look. He didn't care that I didn't love her. I overheard him telling Brittany I was just playing hard to get and to keep trying. She hasn't stopped since."

Gently Chase turned Camara around. His gaze softened when he looked at her. She was certain it was pity because of her tear-filled eyes. Chase pulled her into his arms

186

and pressed her cheek against his chest. "I'm not in love with her, Cam. And she is not my future wife."

Camara sniffed again. In her wildest imagination, Camara never figured that one day she would feel such relief hearing that Chase was a free man. She wasn't sure, but if the way her heart ached when she saw the gorgeous brunette kiss him was any indication of loving someone, then she suspected she might be in love with Chase. The thought terrified her.

Chase tilted her head up and rubbed his thumb under her eyes. "You believe me, don't you?"

"I'm sorr—"

Chase placed his fingers over her lips. "Don't apologize."

"I should have trusted you, Chase. This was my first test in trusting you, and I failed." She pulled back a bit and looked into his eyes. "I'm so sorry. Bear with me."

"Listen, Cam. I understand. After the way I treated you for so many years, I know it's gonna take time to earn your trust." He cupped her face and leaned his face toward hers. "But I have all the time in the world. If you do."

"I do." Her voice sounded husky.

Chase wrapped his arms around her and

lowered his head.

"Oh, honey, isn't young love sweet?"

Camara jerked her head back and turned toward the voice.

"Reminds me of you and me forty years ago." An older couple holding hands stood watching them.

Camara felt her face, neck, and ears heat up.

"Whaddya mean, forty years ago?" The gray-haired gentleman dipped the older lady and kissed her. When he let her go, they laughed and continued on the path.

Camara pictured her and Chase acting like that couple in forty years. Giving herself a mental shake, she wondered why she had even thought that.

She and Chase married? Not likely.

"I'm famished. Let's go get something else to eat. I tossed the other in the trash before I came looking for you," Chase said, looping her hand through his arm. They headed back toward the concession stands in Civitan Park.

"I'm sorry I ruined breakfast."

"You didn't ruin anything. We'll just get something else."

Chase noticed a sign at a nearby concession stand in the park. Funnel cakes, pecan cake, waffles, pancakes, sweet potato biscuits, fresh fruit, boiled peanuts. His stomach growled just reading the list. "Do you like funnel cakes?" He pointed toward the concession stand.

"Like them? I love 'em. Race ya there." She dropped his hand and sprinted off.

She might be wearing a dress, but she was all tomboy. But what a beautiful tomboy she made. He dashed after her, arriving at the same time she did.

Finding a shaded picnic bench, Chase grabbed Camara's hand and lowered his head. "Father, thank You for Your provision. May we never take Your grace for granted. And thank You for mending the fence between me and Camara and for allowing me to spend time with her. In Christ's name, amen."

Camara echoed his amen.

He was so grateful he'd found Camara and was able to explain about Brittany. By the horrified look on Camara's face, he thought he'd never get another chance to be with her. He found the more he was around her, the more he was falling for her. Who would have ever thought even six months ago that he and Camara would be dating?

Chase took a sip of his sweetened tea.

"There's a patriotic-decorated boat parade and a classic auto show today. Would you like to go?" He popped a bite of funnel cake into his mouth.

"Do trucks require fuel to run? Is mud bog racing fun? Do Fords die early deaths?"

If he hadn't noticed her cheeky grin and the teasing glint in her eyes, he might have retaliated. But instead, he pointed his finger at her in warning. "Don't get me started, Ca-mare-oh."

"Okay, okay." She held her hands up. "I surrender." She wiped her mouth with her napkin. "Actually, I never turn down a car show, and a patriotic boat parade sounds great." She broke off a piece of funnel cake and stuffed it into her mouth.

They talked for more than an hour after they finished their funnel cakes and then headed to Civitan Park's parking lot. As they neared, Chase's breath caught in his throat. Classic cars were lined up all over the place. Some of them were jacked up over mirrors, revealing their chrome under-carriage.

A silver 1971 Mach 1 with two black stripes on the hood snatched his attention. He grabbed Camara's hand and headed straight for it. "I've always wanted one of these." The hood was up, and a sign on the hood latch read PLEASE DO NOT TOUCH. Chase longed to hear the Ford's 429 engine come to life.

He noticed a rotund man in his fifties sitting in a chair behind it. How he envied him. Chase had searched for years trying to find a car like this one in good restoration condition. But he'd always called too late. Maybe someday.

Feeling guilty for neglecting Cam, he turned to talk to her. She was gone. He scanned the large area looking for her and spotted her pale yellow dress, so he headed that way.

"Sorry I got carried away back there."

Camara turned and flashed him a dashing smile. "No problem. Sorry I left, but I had to see this."

Chase looked at a purple metal fleck 1934 Ford Coupe all chromed out. This one had Mountain Crusher rims with white raised lettering. After examining it for a few minutes, he turned to Camara. "I knew you had good taste. I wondered how long it would be before you couldn't resist a Ford."

She smiled. "I admit. It's gorgeous. Are you happy now?" Camara walked away and said, "But this one's better." She stopped in front of a baby blue mother-of-pearl and jeweled 1968 Chevrolet Camaro. The opened hood showed off a chromed-out 396 with three deuces on top.

Chase noticed the sign in the window. OWNER: CAMARA CHEVELLE COLE.

Stunned, his gaze flew to Camara. Her face glowed with pride. "This is yours?" He couldn't keep the shock out of his voice.

Camara nodded and smiled. "I customized and restored it all by myself."

Her statement didn't sound prideful.

"You?" he asked, still dumbfounded. "Customized this by yourself?" He knew he sounded like a bumbling idiot, but he had never seen a more incredible car. For a Chevy, that is. He couldn't help but think he had no idea of the depth of her capabilities. He was even more impressed with her and even more in love with her than before. Not wanting his mind to go there, he ducked his head inside the driver's side door and checked out the car's interior. Chase let out a long whistle. He was impressed. It had dark blue diamond tuck upholstery, bucket seats, B&M custom speed shifter, and a full set of street racing instruments. Chase stood and stared in awe before asking, "Don't you have to be here with your car?"

"Normally, yes. But" — she looked bashful — "I wanted to spend time with you today, so when I changed clothes, I asked Daddy if he would come down here. I knew he wanted to anyway. After all, this was his baby before he gave it to me on my eighteenth birthday four years ago. He loves it."

"I love what, honey?" Mr. Cole's voice sounded from behind them.

Chase and Camara spun around.

"Hi, Daddy. Hi, Mom." Camara's parents stood next to them, each one holding a beverage and a cardboard bowl containing fried catfish and hush puppies.

"Hi, honey."

Camara kissed her mother's cheek.

"Hi, Chase," her mother greeted Chase cheerfully. "It's right nice to see you again."

"It sure is," Mr. Cole agreed. He set his drink down then shook Chase's hand.

Chase envied Camara's loving family. The times he'd been around them, they made him feel like family . . . as if they genuinely cared about him. He looked at Camara chatting amiably with her mother. If he had anything to say about it, he would soon be part of this loving family. But first things first. He had to win Camara's heart — which wasn't going to be an easy task.

Later that afternoon, Camara changed into her white capris, blue knit tunic sailor shirt, and her matching blue and white canvas sneakers for the second half of their date. Camara chuckled as she thought about how she looked like a sailor in this outfit. Too bad she hadn't worn it on their first date. She would have fit right in on Chase's pontoon boat. Camara couldn't recall when she'd ever been happier. Spending the whole day with Chase had been like a dream. One from which she didn't want to awaken.

When she heard the doorbell, Camara trotted down the steps and swung the door open. Chase looked handsome in his jeans, green polo shirt, and brown leather loafers.

"Ya ready?" he asked.

"Ready as I'll ever be." She grabbed a light jacket from the coat rack, turned the lock on the door, and shut it behind them.

His hand felt warm against her back as he led her toward his Pantera. "What, no Ford? Are you slipping?"

"Hey, I like other cars, too."

When Chase opened her door, it flipped open upward. "Nice."

"I like it." He winked at her.

On the way to the speedway, they reminisced over the cars they'd seen at the auto show. Chase shared with her how he'd always wanted a Mach 1 but that every time he'd gotten wind of one for sale he'd always been too late. When they neared the speed-way, Chase asked, "Do we park in the contestants' pit or near the grandstands?"

"I asked Erik if he needed any help, and he said no. I think it would be fun to sit in the stands for a change."

"Sounds good." Chase parked the car. "Wait there." He hurried out and ran around to her side, then opened the door for her. Such a gentleman. This guy was full of surprises.

Chase intertwined her fingers with his. Her hand felt small in his larger one. "You hungry?"

"Starved."

"What do ya want?"

"Golden Flake chips and a hot dog sounds good."

Chase held his hand over his heart. "Ah, a lady after my own heart."

They stopped at a concession to get their food. Then they carefully made their way up the wooden steps and sat in the front row.

An hour later, Chase and Camara stood rooting and hollering as Erik flew his mon-ster truck over several dirt mounds and a row of cars. Then he went into a cyclone, spinning around and around. The crowd roared, nearly deafening Camara. She wondered if the people rooted this much for the mud bog racers. With about thirty seconds left of his two minutes, Erik spun around and leaped over an RV, crushing it into shattered pieces. Then he headed toward a semitrailer and flew up over the partially mashed trailer. The Mad Masher landed on its front wheels then flipped over on its top. He'd made the full two minutes.

Camara and Chase rose, clapping and hollering. When the freestyle was over, Erik had won third place. On the way down to the contestants' pit, Chase told Camara he wanted to take her someplace special to watch the fireworks.

"But for the last five years, I've watched the fireworks here."

"Well, not this year." He flashed his best smile.

Down at the contestants' pit, they congratulated Erik and said their good-byes to her family.

Later they pulled up to the same dock where Chase had taken her on their first date. Camara sent him a questioning look.

"Don't worry. I promise you Dad won't show up tonight." His shining eyes and bright smile reassured her. Chase came around, opened her door, and grabbed a bag from behind the seat. With his other hand, he grabbed their jackets.

"C'mon." He shuffled his possessions; then he took her hand and led her to the dock. He stopped in front of a sunburst orange metal-flecked speedboat.

"Wow. Is this yours?"

"Yeah."

"How many boats do you own anyway?"

"Three."

"Only three?" Camara giggled.

"Yeah, this one, the pontoon boat, and . . ." He smiled as he situated the cache he'd brought into the boat. "A twenty-eight-foot cabin cruiser." Chase frowned. "Actually, I bought all these" — he made quote marks with his fingers — " 'toys' when I was looking for happiness. But the joy of having them didn't last as long as I thought it would. That's why there are three. Took me awhile to figure out boats and cars didn't fill what I was trying to fill." He was still fussing with the supplies, not seeming to really be listening to his own words. "I didn't find true fulfillment until I found Christ."

Chase climbed aboard and offered her his hand. He helped her climb on board and motioned to a captain's chair next to the driver's seat. Then he hopped down and untied the dock lines before climbing aboard again.

Chase sat in front of the wheel. "If you get cold, there are blankets under the backseat." Chase fired up the boat. The 327 inboard motor crackled louder than her bogger, sending chills racing through her veins. She gave him a thumbs-up. Chase smiled and backed it away from the dock.

Chase joined the cluster of boats gathering around the barge on Lake Guntersville and dropped the anchor. He helped Camara up, and they walked to the back of the boat.

"Would you like something to drink?"

"Not now, thank you."

Chase sat on the white leather bench and pulled Camara next to him. She snuggled into him and scanned the area. A million twinkling stars sprinkled the sky. Light from the many boats danced along the rippling water. The smell of sulfur smoke mingled with fish filled the air.

Camara glanced at him, but before she had a chance to look away, their gazes locked. The attraction between them sizzled. Chase lowered his head and lightly touched her lips. He pulled back and looked at her as if seeking her permission. Camara closed her eyes and tilted her face upward. Chase's lips found hers in a sweet, tender kiss. A loud boom caused them both to jump. Over a loudspeaker, a deep voice announced, "If I could have your attention please . . . Would everyone please stand and face the barge?"

Camara and Chase stood.

The announcer continued. "We take this time to remember all the men and women who have laid down their lives so that we might enjoy this glorious freedom we're celebrating today. And don't forget to thank God for this blessed nation we live in."

Camara's mouth dropped as they lit a huge fireworks display of the United States flag. Red, white, and blue blazed as "The Star-Spangled Banner" played. Tears pooled in Camara's eyes as overwhelming gratitude washed over her. She thanked God for not only the men and women who gave up their lives, but for those who were still fighting to give her the freedom she sometimes took for granted. And for the freedom she now enjoyed. Eyes closed, she tilted her face toward heaven and thanked God for His grace and mercy and prayed for protection over all those defending this wonderful country she lived in.

When she heard Chase sniff, she opened her eyes and looked into his. Sadness filled them. Before she had a chance to ask him what was wrong, he said on a choked whisper, "My best friend and cousin, James, died in the service a little over a year ago." He swiped his eyes.

Camara remembered how Swamper City had honored his heroic death. Her heart wrenched for Chase . . . and for his loss. "Oh, Chase. I'm so sorry." She pulled him into her arms and held him.

Loud booming caused them both to jerk but, not letting him go, she looked skyward. Colored confetti fell from the sky and reflected in the dark water. Chase wiped his eyes and smiled. Camara had never seen anything so beautiful: Chase's tender heart. His bright smile. And the huge gold, red, white, and blue fireworks drizzling from the sky and fizzling out. "Ooo," she drew out.

Chase sat down and pulled her next to him. She rested her head on his shoulder and stared above them as more fireworks dispelled the Alabama darkness.

Thirty minutes later when the sky lit up with the grand finale, Camara was a bit saddened, knowing her evening was about to come to an end. She loved being cradled in Chase's arms, and she didn't know when she'd had a better time. Who would have ever thought one of her best memories would be made with Chase Lamar? When the fireworks display ended, she whispered,

"Beautiful." She glanced up at Chase, who was staring at her.

"Yeah, she is."

Camara's eyes widened. He was talking about her, not the fireworks. As he leaned down to kiss her, her heart tripped over itself. What was happening to her? Was she falling in love with him?

CHAPTER 15

"Oh, Lolly, my date with Chase yesterday was so romantic." Camara took a bite of her pecan pie and chewed slowly as she contemplated just how much she should reveal to her friend. She didn't want her to tell Stan, who in turn might say something to Chase. Although no other man's kisses had affected her the way Chase's had, and no one else occupied her every thought like Chase did, she was still uncertain of her feelings toward him. Yes, she wanted to trust him. She wanted him to be the man he was on the boat and at the lake house, but was he really that person? The question would not leave her alone.

"What was so romantic?" Lolly tucked her unruly red curls behind her ears.

Camara looked at her friend. "All day long we talked about anything and everything. Then he took me out on his fancy speedboat." She gazed at her coffee. "We snuggled while we watched the fireworks."

Lolly sighed. "Then what happened?" She scooted forward.

Camara looked around the room, then at her friend. Lowering her voice, she added, "Good thing I was sitting when he kissed me because I wouldn't have been able to stand." Camara took a long drink of coffee.

"Sounds like a woman in love." Lolly's eyes looked dreamy.

Camara coughed and sputtered, patting her chest.

Lolly jumped up and started pounding her back. Camara shook her head and waved her off.

"Are you okay?"

"Fine, fine," she rasped, coughing some more.

Lolly handed Camara a glass of water. Camara sipped on it till her throat cleared. "Are you crazy? I am *not* in love with Chase Lamar."

Lolly stared at her. "Uh-huh. If you say so." Her friend's blue eyes twinkled. Lolly peeled off a piece of her honey bun, stuck it in her mouth, and smiled while she chewed.

Camara glanced at her watch. "Will ya look at the time? I'd better get out to Swamper's. I don't wanna be late. Besides, Stan will wonder where you are."

Lolly grabbed Camara's arm. "Just cool your jets, lady. You're always the first one to arrive. Besides" — Lolly glanced at the clock behind the counter at Tooties Gourmet Coffee Shop — "it's only 6:23. You still have plenty of time. And Stan knows exactly where I am. He also knows I'll be home in time to ride with him to Swamper's. Now quit stalling and spill."

"Spill what?"

Lolly sighed heavily. "Are you in love with Chase or what?"

"No. I am not in love with Chase. I told you that. A great kiss doesn't constitute love." Now if only she could convince her heart of that.

"Okay, I'll drop it. For now. But only if you tell me about the rest of your date."

Camara laughed as her friend shoved her plate with her partially eaten honey bun to the side and leaned forward. No wonder Lolly stayed so skinny; she ate like a newborn baby.

Camara finished the last bite of her pie, shoved the plate to the side, and leaned closer to Lolly. She motioned her to come closer with her finger. "No." She stood up, grabbed her yellow cap with the black Chevy emblem, plopped it on her head, and headed out the door.

"Meanie!" Lolly hollered at her.

Camara stepped out to the cloud-covered sky. It looked and smelled like rain. She wished she had grabbed her jacket. Lolly walked up beside her. "You know I'm gonna bug you until you tell me."

Camara smiled at her friend. "Yeah, I know. Tell Stan hello for me." Her brows furrowed. "Lolly." She laid her hand on her arm. "Please don't say anything to Stan." Her gaze fell to the concrete. "About Chase and me. I do have feelings for him, but I don't want Stan to say something to him or anyone else for that matter. This is all really new to me, and we don't need everyone asking questions. Please, promise me you won't say a word."

"I promise." She crossed her fingers over her heart. They hugged. "But remember, it's okay to love him, Cam." With that, her friend walked off to her car and got in. What was that all about? Shrugging the question off, Camara turned to her own vehicle as lightning zigged across the sky, followed by loud thunder. Camara jumped into her Hummer and drove off.

Thirty minutes later, Camara pulled into Swamper Speedway much later than normal. Her heart sped up at the sight of Chase's rig. In a weird way, her feelings for him frightened her. Camara hated that she couldn't seem to gain control over her emotions where Chase was concerned.

Chase stepped out from behind his trailer and glanced her way, motioning for her to park next to him. She sighed. He sure looked good. His blue denim jacket bulged where his biceps were. Those same biceps that held her yesterday.

Camara parked next to him and had barely shut off the engine before Chase opened her door and tugged her out and into his arms. She melted into his embrace.

"What do you think you're doing?" The voice snapped them apart.

Camara spun, nearly losing her balance, and found herself looking into Mr. Lamar's scowling face. *Oh, great.* Camara wanted to hop back into her vehicle and go as far away from his dad as possible. She took a step backward.

Chase draped his arm around her shoulder and tucked her close. "Morning, Dad."

"I told you to stay away from them Coles." He glared at her.

If venomous words had striking power, Camara knew she'd be dead.

"Listen, Chase," Camara said. "I need to unload my truck anyway. I'll talk to you later."

He let her go. She hated being in the middle of family squabbles. Especially this one.

Last night they'd had a deep conversation about how his dad felt about her family. Chase reassured her he refused to be a part of his dad's hatred toward her family. Still, it made her uncomfortable. A part of her never wanted to go near Chase again, but she enjoyed his company way too much to stay away forever. Even the *thought* of staying away from him forever drove fear through the middle of her. Seeing no other option, she did what she always did. "Father, please show me what to do," she whispered as she leaned over to remove a nylon strap from The Black Beast. "Please heal the rift between Chase's dad and my family. Thank You."

From the corners of her eyes, she watched Mr. Lamar get in his vehicle and head toward her. He stopped next to her and rolled down his window. "Stay away from my son, or you'll be sorry. This is the last time I'm gonna warn you." With that, he spun gravel and left. Lightning streaked across the sky and thunder bellowed, making her shiver.

"What did he say to you?" Chase asked from behind her.

Camara spun around. Chase's green eyes held concern. He put his arms around her and hugged her. "Please tell me."

She pulled back. "Can we talk about this later, Chase? I haven't even registered yet, and I have a few things to do." She fought to keep her tone light, but the aggravation she felt came through anyway.

He let her go. "I know a brush-off when I hear one."

Making sure his dad wasn't anywhere around, she laid her hand on his arm. "Look, I'm not giving you the brush-off." He didn't look convinced.

"Don't forget, Cam. In order for us to have a relationship, we have to trust each other. Communication is a part of trusting." He grabbed her hands. Electrical currents shot up her arms, and it wasn't from the lightning flashing around them, either.

"You still wanna be with me, don't you?" The uncertainty in his eyes broke her heart.

She stood on her tiptoes and planted a kiss on his cheek. "Does that answer your question?"

He frowned petulantly. "No."

She pulled his mouth down to hers and kissed him soundly. "Does that answer your question?"

"No," he answered, his eyes sparkling.

"Still not clear."

"Oh, you." She shoved him away.

Chase pulled her back into his arms. Raindrops spotted her cheeks.

She wanted to stay in Chase's embrace, but his father's threat played over and over in her mind. Slowly she pulled away from him so as not to tip him off to her thoughts. "We'd better get our vehicles unloaded."

At that moment, the heavens opened. In the next second, sheets of rain poured on them. Chase grabbed Camara's hand, and they rushed toward his pickup and hopped in.

They sat inside his truck talking for about twenty minutes, his arm around her and she enjoying the safety it provided as they waited for the rain to subside. It took another ten minutes for the sun to peek through the clouds. When the last of the raindrops receded, they both hopped out. "We'd better get unloaded and then go register."

Camara nodded. She quickly unloaded the Beast, and the two of them headed toward the entry booth. By the time they reached the booth, the sun had retaken control of the sky. The thick humid air invaded Camara's lungs.

Chase finished filling out the forms before

Camara. "I'll get us some coffee while you finish."

Camara glanced up from the clipboard. "Thanks." She went back to work on filling out the form. Ten minutes later, she finished. She handed the forms along with her fee to Sam, then perused the area looking for Chase. It sure was taking him a long time to get two cups of coffee. Where was he?

A few minutes later, Chase walked around the entry booth. "Sorry it took so long. They had to make more." He handed her a cup.

Warmth seeped into her hands. "I'm so glad you waited." She picked off the lid and blew into her coffee before taking a sip.

Camara and Chase laughed and joked all the way back to their vehicles. "I'll talk to ya later, Chase. I'm gonna check a few things on The Black Beast."

"Yeah, I have a few things to check, too."

"Bet you have more than a few things." She wrinkled her nose at him. "After all, it is a Ford."

Chase sent her a warning look. Camara winked at him.

When she got back and fired up the Beast, her heart sank at the sound. She put on the emergency brake, grabbed her stepladder, and popped the hood open.

Camara knew from the sound there were loose spark plug wires. She started checking them. Sure enough, three of them were loose. Someone had messed with her truck . . . again. But when? She looked around. Her gaze landed on Chase. She hated where her thoughts were going, but Chase had finished filling out the forms long before she had. And when he'd gone for coffee, it had taken an awfully long time. But then again, she needed to be careful not to judge him. *If we're gonna have a relationship, we have to trust each other.* Chase's words echoed through her mind. Desperately she wanted to.

"Lord, I'm asking You to please, please show me the truth. Expose whoever is doing this." She swallowed hard. "Even if it is Chase."

CHAPTER 16

"Welcome to Swamper Speedway." The announcer's voice over the loudspeaker grabbed Chase's attention.

He'd drawn number one, so he was up first today. Lined up next to him was Bobby-Rae in his beat-up '36 Chevy pickup, Left Behind.

Chase glanced at the contestants' pit and noticed Camara still under the hood of her truck. He knew she'd drawn number three. Whatever she was doing, she needed to hurry up and get it done.

He tried to focus on the flagman, but every time he looked over and saw Camara with the hood still up, his concern increased. His belly sank. Had someone messed with it again?

Two bangs on his Coupe drew his attention. The flagman backed up and guided Chase as he inched his way to the starting line. His heart wasn't in this race. It was with Camara. "Lord, whatever is wrong with The Black Beast, let her get it fixed in time for her run."

It amazed Chase that he no longer cared about beating Camara. He still wanted to do his best, but secretly he wanted her to win. However, knowing how she felt, he'd drive his best and let her earn first place. If he let her win and she found out, she'd be furious with him.

The flag dropped.

Chase flew through the pit. He knew his lightning-fast run stemmed from sheer willpower to go see what was up with Camara's truck.

Without waiting to hear his time, he drove back to his trailer and hopped out. "John, would ya wash this off for me? I'm gonna go see if Camara needs help."

"Sure thing."

"Thanks." Chase sprinted toward Camara. "What's wrong?"

Camara ducked her head out from under the hood and looked at him. Her friendly demeanor and smile were nonexistent. He watched as she studied his face. "Someone messed with my truck again. The spark plug wires are loose, and there's a slit in the vacuum advance hose."

"What?" Chase stood on the tire and

peered at her engine. "What can I do to help you get ready? You're up next."

"I don't have a spare hose, so I'll have to tape it for now. If you'll tighten the spark plug wires while I get some duct tape, that would be great."

He looked around. "Where's Erik? And the rest of your family?"

"There was a problem at the shop. Erik couldn't come." She grabbed the duct tape out of her toolbox. "Tony and Slick had to work, too." She climbed her ladder. "And Mom and Dad are at Civitan Park at the auto show with my car."

"Oh." Chase started tightening the wires.

They worked quickly together and finished just in time to hear the announcer's voice. "Last call for Camara Cole."

Chase gathered the tools and slammed the hood while Camara jumped inside and put on her helmet and gloves. She released the emergency brake. Chase motioned to her that all was clear. She backed up and headed toward the mud pits.

Chase watched her zip her way through the pit. Mud was slung twenty feet or more in the air. Her engine roared, giving him goose bumps. He still loved Fords and always would. But he had to admit The Black Beast was one mean running machine. For a Chevy.

He wondered who had messed with it again. His stomach wrenched as reality struck him. The reason Camara had acted differently toward him was because she probably thought he'd done it again. He knew he should have waited until she was finished before going for coffee. It wouldn't have taken so long if the young girl hadn't tipped over the huge coffeepot. She was lucky it didn't have much in it, or she would have been burned. He'd waited while she made another pot. Camara would probably never believe him. Would she ever learn to trust him? At this point, would he trust him if he were in her position? The only way to prove his innocence was to find out who was behind this.

Camara didn't know what to think. Why would Chase help her if he'd done it in the first place? Or was he just trying to throw her off? No, that didn't make sense. Whoever it was wanted to make her look bad and wanted her to lose. Well, their plan didn't work. Thanks to Chase's help, she didn't miss her run.

On her right, Camara watched as the flagman motioned Stan Morrison forward in One Bad Mudder. Lolly leaned around Stan and waved at Camara.

Camara revved her engine and waved back. It felt strange racing against her best friend's husband. Well, best friend or not, she had to do her best. She had to show whoever was behind this, making her look bad, that she wasn't a quitter. Her hands shook so badly she could barely grip the steering wheel, and her insides shook equally as bad. *I just have to win. I'll show you, whoever you are. You won't get the best of me. Oh, Lord. Why don't they just leave me alone? All I ever wanted to do was race and fix and build trucks. But no, they have to use my gender against me.* She snorted. *Like I can help that.*

The flag dropped.

Camara jerked her foot off the brake, floored the gas pedal, and dove into the pit. Mud covered her windshield as The Black Beast flew through the pit. She hung her head out the window and watched the side of the pit until she felt her truck leap out of the pit and land with a light thud. "What a rush!" Mud dripped from her arm.

Back at the contestants' pit, she ripped off her helmet, gloves, and harness. Chase yanked her door open and pulled her into a hug.

"What a run! You've heard of Jesus walking on water? Well, girl, you just walked on mud." He swung her around and planted a kiss on her muddy lips.

As his lips molded over hers, all doubts vanished. There was no way Chase had messed with her truck.

When Chase raised his head, Camara giggled.

"What's so funny?"

"Now your lips are muddy, too." She reached up and ran her finger over his lip. Amid the grit, her fingers felt soft and warm. She stood on her tiptoes and kissed him, making his lips tingle.

They didn't hear the boots on the gravel. The voice was the first indication either of them had that they had an audience. "What would your father say if he could see you now?"

Camara jerked back. Bobby-Rae stood glaring at her.

"My father would tell me to do it again," she replied curtly.

"Not you. Him." He nodded toward Chase.

"What does it matter to you? And how do you know what my dad would think?" Who did this guy think he was anyway?

Big burly Bobby-Rae's cheeks flushed.

"I . . ." He shifted his weight. "I heard him tell Camara that she'd better stay away from you, or she'd be sorry."

Chase looked at Camara as concern twisted through him. "Is that true?"

She nodded then glared at Bobby-Rae. "Don't you have anything better to do? Like go play in traffic or something?"

His smirk turned to a frown. He opened his mouth as if to say something, looked at Chase, then whirled and stormed off.

Camara shook her head. "He sure has changed. It's kinda sad. Before people started requesting me to fix their vehicles at work, Bobby-Rae and I used to have a lot of fun and were even friends. Now he's downright hateful since I turned him down." She jerked her head toward Bobby-Rae and looked at Chase.

"Turned him down for what?"

"Never mind."

The reality of what she wasn't saying crashed over Chase. Bobby-Rae must have asked her out, and she had turned him down. That explained why he was making her life miserable.

"Is it true what Bobby-Rae said? Did my dad threaten you again?"

She took three steps away from him to the power washer, but she didn't pick it up. "Yeah."

Chase stepped over to her and gathered Camara's hands in his. "Don't let my dad bother you, Cam. His bark is worse than his bite." As the words left Chase's mouth, a pit settled in his stomach. He no longer knew what his dad was capable of. Lately his father's obsession to ruin the Coles looked more and more dangerous. An awful thought slid through him. Certain his dad was somehow involved with Camara's truck incidents, he knew he had to figure out a way to prove his suspicions.

"I won't," Camara said softly. "I just feel bad that he hates us so much."

Chase was more than surprised when she wrapped her arms around him and laid her head against his chest. He drew her close and kissed the top of her head. Love for this woman compelled him to protect her. Even against his own father.

"I'm hungry. How about you?" Camara asked, moving out of his arms.

"Do you think it's safe to leave The Black Beast?"

"I'll ask Lolly to keep an eye on it."

Camara grabbed her cell phone from her Hummer and called her friend. A minute later, she disconnected the call.

"Okay, let's go."

At the concession stand, they each ordered fried chicken, nachos, and sweetened tea.

Camara set her food down and straddled the picnic bench. Chase lowered himself beside her, grabbed her hand, and bowed his head. "Father, we thank You for this food, and we ask You to bless it. And, Lord, please expose the person who's sabotaging Camara's truck. In Christ's name, amen."

Camara's heart chirped a happy tune. She truly believed if Chase was guilty, he would not have prayed about it.

"What are you smiling about?"

Returning his smile, she answered, "Nothing. Nothing at all." She leaned over and boldly kissed him.

CHAPTER 17

The last day of the season's mud bog race dawned more perfect than if Camara had ordered it herself. Only one small cloud dotted the blue sky arching over the grandstand, which sported the white flag with the red Saint Andrew's cross. Just like her home state, it was simple yet etched in dignity. Over it flew the American flag, which brought goose bumps to her arms with the memory of Chase standing on a boat, his hand over his heart and tears in his eyes. Strange how even the smallest of things could make her think about him. Several people were already seated in the grandstands. More than forty mud bog trucks had showed up today for the final runs of the season.

Not threatened by any of them, Camara smiled. She knew she still had to deal with her prideful attitude and the need to prove herself, but if she beat Chase's time today, she'd be Swamper Speedway's mud bog champion. If not, they would most likely tie for first.

Wanting everything to be in tip-top shape, she popped open the hood, grabbed her stepladder, and bent over the engine.

Weeks had passed since Camara and Chase had started seeing each other regularly. Chase discovered they had more in common than just their love of building and racing bog trucks, fixing and restoring vehicles, and God. They openly shared their thoughts, their feelings, and their dreams, which happened to crisscross each other very nicely. Greatest of all, though, was that Camara now trusted him.

Numerous times Chase had fought the urge to tell Camara he loved her. By her response to their conversations and his kisses, and by the way she looked at him, he thought she loved him, too. But until he knew for sure how she felt about him, he'd wait to voice his feelings.

Chase leaned across the seat of his '34 Ford Coupe feeling around on the floorboard for the fuse he'd dropped. Hearing his father's lowered voice, he froze, listening.

"Did you take care of it this time?"

"I sure did." The voice sounded familiar, but Chase couldn't quite place it.

"Did anybody see you?"

"Not a soul. This time should do the trick."

Chase heard a vile laugh that made his blood turn cold.

"Miss Hoity-Toity will finally be knocked off her high horse. And I'm gonna be right there when she is."

Chase strained to hear above the vehicles revving their engines around him.

"No one will get hurt, will they?" his father asked.

"What do you care? You paid me to do a job, and I did it."

"I paid you to make sure Chase won."

What? Chase couldn't believe what he'd just heard. How could his dad do that to him? Chase swallowed hard against the bitter bile rising up his esophagus. The urge to hop out and say something overwhelmed him, but he wanted to hear the whole conversation.

"He will. I made sure of that. In fact, I should pay you." The man's chuckle sounded demonic. "I've waited a long time to watch her fall flat on her face. Every time someone came into the shop, they'd always ask for Camara as if she were the only one good enough —"

Chase had heard enough. He flew out of the Mud Boss, infuriated at the very thought of anyone hurting Camara. His dad and Bobby-Rae stood a foot from his Coupe gawking at him. Chase seized the front of Bobby-Rae's shirt with his fists. "What did you do to Camara's truck?"

"Wouldn't you like to know?" he sneered.

"Tell me now, or I'll —"

"You'll what?" Bobby-Rae challenged. "Besides, it's too late to do anything about it now." The contemptuous way Bobby-Rae said it made Chase's stomach clench.

Before Chase could respond, his father asked, "What did you do to it, Bobby-Rae?" A frown marred his face.

"Let's just say she won't be doing any racing or anything else for quite some time."

His dad moved closer to Chase. "I didn't hire you to hurt her, only to make sure she didn't win."

His suspicions had been confirmed. But the very idea of his dad hiring someone to sabotage The Black Beast caused Chase's mind to nearly blow a gasket. His thoughts whirled with the ramifications of what Bobby-Rae could have done to Camara's truck.

"What did you do?" His father's commanding voice demanded an answer.

Chase fought the urge to run to Camara right then, but he figured it was best if he found out just exactly what Bobby-Rae had done.

A look of pride and a snide grin filled Bobby-Rae's face. "You told me to keep a close eye on what they do. Well, I learned one very important detail. Before starting the truck, Erik never checks the nitrous oxide switch cuz it ain't never turned on until Camara's lined up at the pit. So about an hour ago, I flipped it on."

"You what?" Chase's gaze darted toward the far end of the contestants' pit. His heart stopped beating. The hood was raised on The Black Beast, and all Chase could see was Camara's short legs and backside. His stomach lodged in his throat. "Lord, no!" She was leaning over the engine, and Erik was inside the cab. Why of all days had he been forced to park clear on the opposite end of the pits from her?

Without waiting for more explanation, Chase tossed Bobby-Rae to the side and took off at a dead run. "Camara!" he screamed at the top of his lungs. However, with all the mud bog vehicles revving their engines, the music blaring from the PA system, and people's laughter, she didn't even look his way. Chase slipped on the loose gravel and landed on his hands and knees. Ignoring the pain in his legs, he jumped up and willed his legs to go faster. "Erik, don't start the truck," he yelled. "Erik!"

Standing on her stepladder in front of the fender well, Camara hollered, "Okay, Erik, fire her up."

Kaboom! Her head jerked up, slamming against the hood. Pain ricocheted through her hands, her face, and the back of her head. The world spun, and then everything turned black.

It was as if Chase were watching a horror movie playing in slow motion. Metal particles flew from Camara's engine. Camara slumped to the ground next to the fender, limp as a rag doll.

"Caa-m-a-rr-aa!" His heart slammed against his ribs.

Chase and Erik reached her at the same time. She lay crumpled on her side in a heap.

"Cammy?" Erik's voice shook. "Oh no! No! Please no!"

Erik reached for her, but Chase clutched his arms. "Don't move her." His gaze landed on the back of Camara's head. Her beautiful blond hair was soaked with blood. And her arms had blood trailing down them. When his gaze landed on a piece of metal sticking out of her arm, Chase swallowed as he fought the urge to throw up.

Oh, God, please let her be okay.

A crowd gathered. Over the loudspeaker, Chase heard the announcer's voice. "We need the medics to the contestants' pit immediately. There's been an accident." A hush rushed through the grandstands.

He looked back at Camara's still form.

Mr. and Mrs. Cole knelt beside Camara and prayed for her. Comforted by their presence and prayers, peace washed over Chase.

The ambulance attendants arrived, and as one, everyone stepped back to let them through.

God, please don't let anything happen to her. I need her. Chase drew in a long, shaky breath and slowly exhaled, fighting to keep the fear from overpowering him as he watched them slowly roll her onto the loose gravel. Her face was streaked with oozing crimson streams. *Oh, God, help. I love her.*

In the middle of fear, anger snapped like lightning. None of this would have happened if it wasn't for his father's hatred toward the Coles . . . and his lack of confidence in Chase. Chase couldn't believe how much that thought hurt. For years he'd tried desperately to win his father's approval, only to fail over and over again.

"I'm sorry, son." Chase felt his father's hand on his shoulder. He looked over to see his father's repentant face. His being sorry wouldn't help Camara. Chase couldn't deal with him right now. As angry as he was, he knew it would be best if he just walked away until he had a chance to calm down. Besides, all he wanted to do was get to the hospital as soon as possible. He spun around. With his father on his heels, he headed toward his pickup and quickly unhitched the trailer.

"Where you going?" his father asked. "You have a race to finish."

Chase shook his head in utter disbelief. He must have imagined the look of repentance on his dad's face. He whirled, facing his father. "Winning is everything to you, isn't it? You don't even have the decency to feel bad that Camara is on her way to the hospital right now because of your obsession with destroying the Coles and winning. I hope you're happy now." He dug in his pockets. "Here are the keys to the Mud

Boss. You wanna win so bad, you drive. I've got more important things to do." He started his Ford Power Stroke pickup, ground it into gear, and spun out.

On the way to the hospital, he prayed, "Lord, how can I ever forgive my father for what he's done to Camara? I know I'm to show him the love of Christ, but how do you deal with somebody like him? His obsession could have killed Camara."

He closed his eyes at the thought that he wasn't sure it hadn't. At the sound of a horn honking, his eyelids flew open. He swerved back into his own lane and mouthed an apology to the lady driver shaking her fist at him.

At the hospital, Chase parked his truck and sprinted into the emergency room entrance. Camara's dad and Erik were talking to a staunch-looking nurse.

Chase stopped several yards away from them. Did he have a right to be here, knowing his dad was responsible? They hadn't seen him yet. However, before he had a chance to leave, Erik and Mr. Cole spotted him and walked over to him.

"How's she doing?"

"The doctor's in with her now. Mom said she'd let us know as soon as she knows anything." Erik's eyes glistened, and worry lines etched his forehead. "This is all my fault. I should have checked everything before I started it up."

He couldn't let Erik blame himself, knowing the truth. "I need to tell y'all something." At their nodding assent, Chase motioned for them to follow him. How would Erik and Mr. Cole feel about him once they found out the truth?

They went to the empty waiting area and sat. Event by event, Chase explained everything.

Erik shook his head. "I know your dad hates us, but this has got to stop."

"It will."

Chase's gaze darted toward the sound of his father's voice. "What are you doing here?" Chase ground out. "Haven't you done enough damage for one day?"

Mr. Cole laid his hand on Chase's arm and signaled Chase with a slight shake of his head.

God, help me here. For a single second, he thought about Camara's counting-to-ten tactic, but that thought just slammed more anger into him.

However, seeing his father's haggard face — bowed with guilt and remorse — softened him. His father looked at Erik and extended his hand.

Erik stood and accepted his proffered hand.

Next he extended his hand to Mr. Cole. Chase couldn't have been more shocked if a lightning bolt had hit him. If he hadn't seen it with his own eyes, he'd never have believed it. His dad was actually shaking the hand of not just one Cole, but two.

"I know it's too late to say I'm sorry." His dad looked at the floor and released Mr. Cole's hand. "But I am." He looked at Erik and Mr. Cole and then at Chase. "More than y'all will ever know." Mr. Lamar motioned to a nearby seat. "May I?"

Mr. Cole nodded. "Please."

When all three were seated, his dad looked at Chase then at Mr. Cole. "I never meant for Camara to get hurt, Landon. I know that's hard to believe considering how I've done everything in my power to make you pay for what you did to me." He rubbed the back of his neck.

Chase darted a glance in Mr. Cole's direction, scoping out his response. All he saw was love, mercy, and compassion. He no longer wondered how Mr. Cole felt after he heard the news that his dad was behind Camara's accident. Chase forced back the tears stinging his eyes and focused his attention on his dad.

"Ever since that day in our senior year of college" — his dad's gaze looked distant as if he'd slid back in time — "when that pro football scout offered me a job after I graduated from college, I couldn't wait to tell you and Cassandra. But when I found my girlfriend with her arms around my best friend's neck and the two of you kissing, I felt betrayed and angry. All I remember is punching you in the face several times and then being slammed into the ground. When I woke up in the hospital, the doctor informed me I'd suffered a blow to the head and had been in a coma for nearly three days. Like it was no big deal, the doctor said, 'Sorry, young man. But pro football isn't in your future. No one can risk hiring you after a head injury like this.' "

His dad closed his eyes briefly then looked right at Mr. Cole. "Every time I watched a football game and was reminded of what I'd lost, all I wanted was to make you pay for destroying my career. Because you were always big into Chevys and I was always into Fords, when you bought a Chevrolet dealership, I figured the one way to get even with you was to buy a Ford dealership and take business away from you."

He sat, shaking his head, his gaze on the floor. "And every time you bought another dealership, I did. When that didn't work, I tried everything I could think of to make your business and your kids look bad. But nothing worked. So when I overheard Bobby-Rae telling another guy that he'd had it up to his scalp with Camara Cole and he'd do anything to make her look bad, I saw another opportunity to get even with you." He shook his head. "But I never meant for this to happen." Seeing his superior, I'm-in-control father broken melted Chase's anger.

"Barry, I'm so sorry." Mr. Cole exuded compassion. "There's nothing I can say or do to change what's happened. But I'm asking you to hear my side. Please?"

Mr. Lamar gave a quick nod.

"You know how Cassandra was the biggest flirt on campus and kissed any man in a football jersey."

Mr. Lamar briefly closed his eyes and nodded.

"Well, that night she'd had one too many to drink. I told her she needed to go home and sleep it off. She asked if I'd join her. Before I had a chance to respond, she threw her arms around my neck and kissed me." He swiped his lips. "When you grabbed me and started decking me, all I wanted to do was stop you from using my face as a punching bag. I never meant for you to get hurt when I tackled you to the ground." He moved his head from side to side in slow motion. "I never saw that rock." The look in Mr. Cole's eyes when he gazed at his dad begged him to believe he was telling the truth. "I tried so many times to tell you I didn't betray you, but I couldn't get you to really hear what I was saying." Sadness dimmed his eyes. "I've always loved you, Barry. Like a brother. Still do."

His dad's eyes widened. He shook his head. "I should have read the letters you sent me and taken your calls. But I couldn't. I blamed you, and I wanted to hurt you like you hurt me. I was wrong. And now Camara is paying for my bitterness." He ran his hand over his face.

Erik pulled himself to his feet. "Speaking of Camara, I wanna check on her."

"Me, too." Mr. Cole stood.

Chase and his dad rose. "If y'all don't mind, I'd like to go, too."

"Of course." Mr. Cole didn't hesitate to agree, much to Chase's relief.

Chase turned to his dad. He grabbed him and hugged him. "I love you, Dad." Chase pulled back. "Do you wanna come with us?"

"No." Mr. Lamar shook his head. "I'm tired. I need to go home and rest." He shook

Erik's and Mr. Cole's hands. "Thanks for understanding, Landon. I'm really sorry about everything."

When his father turned and strode off with his shoulders hunched, Chase wondered if he was really going to be okay. In fact, he wondered if any of them would ever be okay again.

CHAPTER 18

Right before closing time, two weeks after her accident, Camara stood outside Mr. Lamar's main Ford dealership office. *Lord, give me the courage to talk to him.* She drew in a deep breath and knocked softly on his door, almost hoping he wouldn't be there.

"Mr. Lamar, may I speak with you, please?" Camara trembled as she pushed the door open. It wasn't from fear of him but fear of him rejecting her.

"Camara." Shock and uncertainty marred the older man's features. He slowly rose. "Come on in." His voice quavered.

She couldn't believe how haggard he looked. In fact, he looked worse than she did with the jagged gash that now made a diagonal across her forehead. Camara walked into his office and closed the door. He stood in front of his chair, facing her. Camara drew in a deep breath.

"Chase told you everything, didn't he?"

Boy, he didn't waste any time. "Yes, he did. But that's not why I'm here." At his puzzled look, Camara continued. "I wanted to let you know that I won't be pressing any charges."

She had wanted to tell Bobby-Rae the same thing, but he'd skipped town. With all her heart, Camara wished she could have convinced Swamper Speedway not to press charges against either man, but they had anyway. The trial was pending. With any luck, Mr. Lamar would only have to pay a hefty fine and do community service.

Mr. Lamar's eyes widened, and relief flooded his features, making him instantly look ten years younger. It was the first time Camara had seen him speechless. He motioned for her to sit down. Camara lowered herself into a mahogany leather chair. It squeaked as she crossed her legs. "I came to let you know I understand why you paid Bobby-Rae to sabotage my truck." The words, though skittish and slow, were coming easier than she had imagined they would.

"It all seems so foolish now." Mr. Lamar's gaze roamed over her singed, scab-streaked arms and then over the gash on her head. "I can't tell you how sorry I am."

Camara's heart went out to him. She'd

never seen him look so vulnerable. Most of the time he reminded her of Goliath the giant: in control, prideful, powerful, arrogant, and extremely intimidating. But not now. Not today.

"I understand," Camara said softly. "Winning was everything to me, too. My obsession with proving I was just as good a driver and mechanic as any man drove me to do some foolish things." She looked down at her lap as shame washed over her afresh. "My foolish pride nearly cost me my life . . ." Drawing in a shaky breath, she looked at him. "Twice."

Her arm itched where the stitches had just been removed. She subconsciously rubbed it lightly.

Mr. Lamar's gaze seemed anchored to the table. "I never meant for you to get hurt."

"I know. Chase told me."

He never looked up.

She uncrossed her legs and rose. "Well, I've taken up enough of your time."

Instantly he looked at her and walked around the desk. "Thank you for not pressing charges, Camara. And for being so understanding."

Camara chuckled. "Don't thank me, Mr. Lamar. Thank the Lord. If it wasn't for Him humbling me and showing me three very important lessons, I'd still be a prideful brat."

He smiled and paused. "And what lessons are those?"

Surprised that he asked, Camara responded, "One . . . pride only brings destruction and misery to yourself and to those you love." She darted a quick glance at the ceiling. "I learned that the hard way." He nodded his agreement. "Two . . . I was so obsessed with proving to everyone I could build and race as good as any man that I neglected to work on what was really important: building inner character and walking in love." She stopped and let that sink in. When understanding crossed his face, she went on. "And three . . . it's not about winning. It really is about how you play the game."

He nodded, and a hint of a smile flashed through his eyes.

"Well, thank you for seeing me, Mr. Lamar." She turned and started to walk away.

"Camara?"

She stopped and turned. "Yes?"

The humility on his face showed how hard it was for him to look at her. "You'll never know how much your coming here today means to me. Thank you."

"You're welcome." She smiled. With her heart lighter than it had been in weeks, she nearly floated to her car.

Chase and Camara walked into the sanctuary of the church and sat in the last pew. Everyone came up to Camara and asked how she was doing. Chase knew she still had headaches a lot and that her arms and head were still tender where the burns and gashes were.

He looked up at the enormous royal blue banner hanging on the wall at the opposite end of the pew. In gold letters, he read 1 Corinthians 13:4–8: "Love suffers long and is kind; love does not envy; love does not parade itself, is not puffed up; does not behave rudely, does not seek its own, is not provoked, thinks no evil; does not rejoice in iniquity, but rejoices in the truth; bears all things, believes all things, hopes all things, endures all things. Love never fails."

He looked at Camara and smiled. She slipped her soft hand into his and returned his smile.

Although the sign spoke of God, Camara had suffered long at Chase's hands, his father's hands, and the hands of her fellow workers and racers. She had every right to be angry with all of them, but instead she chose to walk in love. She forgave them all, and she'd even gone to his father's work and shown *him* love. Love for her radiated from the center of Chase's soul.

Camara's eyes widened as she glanced past Chase's shoulder. "Mr. Lamar!"

Chase jerked his head around. "Dad! What are you doing here?"

"I came to see what my family found so fascinating." He extended his hand toward Camara. "Hello, Camara. Good to see you again."

Chase was speechless. All he could do was stare.

With a glint in his eye, his father smiled. "Aren't you going to ask me to sit down?"

Chase had never seen his father like this before. Camara tugged on his hand and moved down. "Oh . . . um . . . yeah."

His father's smile widened as he sat down next to Chase.

During the service, the pastor talked about God's powerful love and forgiveness. And how there was nothing too big or too bad that God would not forgive. Chase glanced at his father. Tears trickled down his cheeks. Chase silently interceded for his father's soul to be saved.

At the end of the service, the pastor asked anyone who wanted to be forgiven of their sins and to accept God's free gift of love and salvation to come forward. Without hesitation, Chase's dad stood and walked down the aisle. Dumbstruck, Chase looked at Camara. Her face was wet with tears. Part of his prayers had just been answered. Now the only unanswered prayers remaining were for his parents to get back together again and for Camara to say yes to his proposal.

Everyone stood around Mr. Lamar congratulating and welcoming him into the family. Camara was the first to hug him.

He whispered next to her ear. "It's all because of you, you know. Your actions yesterday showed me what true Christianity is all about. Love and forgiveness." His gaze caught hers as he gently patted her back. "Thank you."

Camara's heart swelled. A shudder vibrated through her at the thought of what might have happened if she would have been vengeful and pressed charges.

Outside the church, under the hot Alabama sun, Mr. Lamar stopped and faced them. "This stuff is new to me. But will you two pray for me?" He looked at Chase. "I'm going straight to your mother's place and ask her to forgive me for being such a prideful fool." He smiled at Camara then looked back at Chase. "And to see if she'll take me back."

"Where are we going?" Camara asked Chase for the third time.

"You're not very patient, are you?" he asked with a smile in his voice.

"No, I'm not."

Twenty minutes later, Chase turned at the Swamper Speedway entrance. Camara looked at him and frowned. "Why are we coming here? Nothing's scheduled for today."

"You'll see." Chase stopped the vehicle behind the wall of dogwood trees and looked at Camara. "Close your eyes and don't peek until I tell you, okay?"

Camara let out a slow, dramatic breath. Chase chuckled. "Such a drama queen, you are. Just close your eyes."

Camara slapped his arm and closed her eyes. Chase couldn't resist. He leaned toward her and gave her a long, lingering kiss. When he pulled away, Camara slowly opened her eyes with raised brows. "Is that why you wanted my eyes closed?"

"Nope." He smiled. "I just couldn't resist those pouty lips. Now promise me you won't open your eyes again until I say it's okay."

Camara gave him a pretend annoyed look; then she nodded and pinched her eyes shut.

Chase drove down the long lane toward Swamper Speedway and pulled into the center of the oval racetrack. "Don't forget. No matter what, don't open your eyes, okay?"

"I got it already." She giggled.

After shutting the truck off, Chase got out and grabbed her hand and helped her out. "Don't look, okay?"

"I won't." Her voice sounded impatient.

Chase gently led her up the three steps into the white lattice gazebo.

"Don't move or open your eyes yet." He let go of her hand, lit the candle, filled their glasses, and turned on the hidden video camera in the corner; then he went back to her. Making sure he was out of the camera's way, Chase stood off to the side and fixed his gaze on Camara's face. "You can open your eyes now."

Camara opened her eyes and gasped. She was standing inside the most beautiful white lattice gazebo she'd ever seen. Lined along the walls of the gazebo were vases filled with hundreds of yellow daisies. Her favorite flower. For as long as she could remember, her daddy had given her a bunch of yellow daisies every time she was sad or discouraged. He said they would cheer her up. And they did. A smile lifted the corners of her lips.

She continued perusing the gazebo. In the middle was a small round table with a white lacy tablecloth draped over it and two white wicker chairs. In the center of the table sat a ring of yellow daisies wrapped around a tall crystal votive cup with a yellow candle inside. Two silver covered dishes with yellow linen napkins and silverware were set on the table, along with two crystal goblets filled with a clear sparkly beverage.

She looked at him as awe and thankfulness filled her soul. "Oh, Chase. It's beautiful." Her forehead wrinkled. "What's the occasion?"

Chase stood for one more second, cleared his throat, then dropped to one knee in front of her. Her heart leaped out of her chest, and her stomach did the dance of a million butterflies.

"Camara Chevelle Cole, I love you with all my heart, and I hope you love me, too. Will you marry me?" The hopeful look on his face crushed her. Didn't he know she loved him? Of course not. She'd only implied it, not spoken it. But then again, neither had he — until now.

"Oh, Chase, I love you, too." She nodded so fast she thought her neck might snap. "Of course I'll marry you." She tugged his arms until he stood. Carefully she placed her arms around him and kissed him soundly.

When she pulled back, Chase reached inside his pocket and pulled out a model of a Dodge pickup. Camara raised her brows.

He opened the hood. Inside lay a glistening daisy-shaped ring with a large diamond in the center surrounded by yellow diamonds. "Oh, Chase." They were the only two words she could find in her heart. Tears pooled in her eyes as she looked up at him. "I've never seen anything so beautiful in my life."

Chase took the ring out and slid it on her left ring finger. After a kiss that left her weak in the knees, she glanced at the Dodge model still in his hand. "But, what's with the Dodge?"

"Well." He took a step back and looked at her. "I figured you'll always be a Chevy lover. And I'll always be a Ford fan. So, to stop any fighting before it gets started, I thought we should compromise and build a Dodge mud bog truck together and call it . . ." He turned the model sideways until she could see the name on the door.

Camara threw her head back and laughed.
"X-Rivals . . ." She drew out the last word
in a deep masculine voice. "Domination."

EPILOGUE

Camara stepped out of her parents' car and looked around. Of all the fancy places in town where they could have gotten married, they chose Swamper Speedway. Both sets of parents thought they were nuts, but to Chase and Camara, this place was and always would be special.

The early spring day felt hand chosen, as well. The endless blue sky seemed to smile down its approval on them. The dogwood trees on the east end of Swamper Speedway were in full bloom, a symbol of a new beginning, just like her and Chase.

The parking lot was filled to capacity with their guests' vehicles. At the far end of the contestants' pit, she spotted Chase's truck and smiled. Today she would become Mrs. Chase Lamar. Her insides trembled with excitement.

"Come on, dear. You don't want Chase to see you," her mother coaxed. Arm in arm, they sashayed toward the makeshift tent dressing room. Inside, Camara stared in the mirror. Her mother stood behind her, shaking her head.

"Well, one thing's for certain. There's never been another bride anywhere dressed like you." Her mom smiled. "Somehow I imagined my only daughter's wedding differently. I envisioned white lace, long sleeves, a beaded dress with a long train and veil." Her mother chuckled. "Not loose-fitting white coveralls, white steel-toed work boots, and a white lacy cap with a yellow Chevy emblem and a waist-length veil."

Her mother turned Camara around and kissed her cheek. "I can honestly say, though . . . this outfit definitely fits you."

"Cammy, can I come in?" Lolly's voice sang from outside.

"Come in."

"Hurry up, Lolly. Only ten minutes until the ceremony," her mother playfully chastened. When Lolly entered, Camara's mom did a slow inspection of her attire, as well. "I like the coveralls."

Behind her mother's back, Camara winked at Lolly.

Her mother turned back and pulled Camara into a hug. "I love you, sweetheart. See you out there." She turned and left.

Camara and Lolly burst out laughing. "Won't they all be surprised?"

Lolly reached into her satchel and handed Camara a portion of their surprise. Camara tucked them in the pockets of her coveralls and peeked outside through a small slit. She stared at the exact gazebo where Chase had proposed to her. Almost everything was the same. Yellow daisies lined the wall, and a small round table sat in the middle. But instead of the crystal votive cup with the yellow candle in the center, a four-foot-tall trophy, the one she and Chase had won with their tied points, stood in the middle. They had opted to forgo a tiebreaker and had chosen instead to share the title. Chase and Camara had asked Dan if he would agree to have their winning trophy sport The Black Beast on the left, the Mud Boss on the right, and above those two the X-Rivals Domination Dodge truck. Dan thought it was a great idea and gladly obliged.

She gazed at Erik, standing front and center, waiting for Chase and the pastor to make their entrance. As Chase's best man, Erik was the one person who had been there for both of them through even the rough patches. She wondered where she would be without her beloved brother's constant support and his belief in both her and Chase.

"You ready, Camara?" her dad called from outside the small tent.

"Yes, Daddy."

The band started playing the Beach Boys' song "409." "That's your cue, Lolly."

Camara moved out of the way. Lolly pulled the drawstring on the tent opening, lifting it like a swag.

They picked up their daisy bouquets held together with new spark plug wires. Camara watched her guests' mouths fall open as Lolly strolled out of the tent and up the yellow runway. Inwardly she giggled.

When Lolly took her place up front, "The Wedding March" started.

Camara clutched her father's arm tighter. Her knees felt weak.

"You okay, baby girl?"

"I'm fine, Daddy."

"Have I told you lately how proud I am of you?" His eyes registered the love he had for her. "You've grown into a fine young lady."

Camara looked at her coveralls and then up at her daddy. They both chuckled.

When they stepped in view of the guests, gasps rippled through the crowd. She looked at Chase. There was surprise for only a second, then a smile so broad she thought his face would crack from the strain to his lips. She sent him a quick smile and a wink.

Three steps down the aisle, Camara stopped. Her father looked at her with concern.

"Would you hold this, please, Daddy?" She handed him her bouquet.

Camara leaned over. Making sure she didn't mess up her grease-free, French-manicured nails, she removed the steel-toed work boots and exposed her bare, light yellow pedicured toes. She reached into the pockets of her coveralls, pulled out a pair of white strap sandals, and placed them next to her feet. Then she unzipped her coveralls, pulled the sleeves off her shoulders, and stepped out of them. While slipping her feet inside the sandals, she heard her guests gasping again, followed by oohs and aahs.

When she straightened, everyone was smiling, and several were shaking their heads and laughing.

Underneath the coveralls, she had on a white, lacy-sleeved, beaded wedding dress that hugged her tiny waist. The scarf-style hem flowed freely to her knees in the front and hung to her calves in the back. Camara caught her mother's glistening eyes as she dabbed at them with her white linen hankie. Camara smiled at her mother then signaled Lolly to step out of her coveralls. She looked beautiful in her light yellow scarf-style dress.

"Come on, Daddy." She looped her arm in his, satisfied that everything was now perfect. As they headed toward Chase, who looked drop-dead gorgeous in his black-tailed tuxedo and light yellow shirt, she captured his approving gaze and willed her eyes to show him how much she loved him.

After Pastor Stephans had them repeat their vows, he said, "You may now kiss the bride."

Chase's lips melded with hers in a heart-stopping, knee-buckling kiss. His grip tightened as he held her up. When they pulled apart, Pastor Stephans announced, "I'm pleased to present to you Mr. and Mrs. Chase Lamar."

Camara looked at her guests. Her gaze landed on her new father- and mother-in-law and sister-in-law, Heather. Mr. Lamar winked at her and then smiled lovingly at his wife. Camara refused to cry. Mrs. Lamar had profusely told Camara how grateful she was for her part in her husband coming to the Lord. And how happy she was to be living under the same roof again with the man she had never stopped loving . . . or praying for.

Camara squeezed her newly wedded husband's hand and smiled at him. Now he had two loving families. And so did she.

After they cut the cake, Camara grabbed Chase's hand and tugged him outside the huge tent. His steps thumped next to hers, trying to keep up. "Where are we going?"

"You're not very patient, are you?" She winked at him.

Chase snickered. "Already throwing my words back at me, are you? This doesn't bode well."

"Close your eyes, and don't open them until I tell you it's okay."

"Again with my words."

Camara stopped and put her hands over his eyes to force them closed. "Okay, don't open them until I tell you."

"Okay, I get it." Chase imitated her annoyed tone.

Camara pulled the soft car cover off and tossed it on the ground.

"Okay, you can open your eyes now."

Chase's eyes bulged with shock. "What's this?" he asked, gaping at the silver 1971 Mach 1 he'd seen at the car show.

"My wedding present to you."

"What? When? How?" Chase stammered, running his hands over the metal.

"When you said you'd been trying to find one for years, I got the guy's number and offered him a deal he couldn't refuse."

Shaking his head slowly, Chase pulled Camara into his arms. "Thank you, sweetheart." He kissed her.

"You're welcome," she whispered against his lips.

Several hours later, toward evening, Camara slipped back into her coveralls. They said good-bye to their guests and strolled hand in hand toward the Dodge X-Rivals Domination bog truck.

"I get to drive," Camara said.

"No, I'm driving."

"No fair," Camara argued as they continued their way toward the truck and the mud pit. "Why should you go first?"

"Cuz I'm the man." He winked.

"Well, haven't you ever heard of" — she smiled coyly — "ladies first?"

Chase handed her the keys. "Okay, you win."

"I sure did." She kissed him. "I won the best man in the whole world." She handed him the keys and ran around to the passenger's side and hopped in.

They glanced at their guests watching them from a distance and waved. Then each grabbed their harnesses.

With tin cans and streamers hanging all over the Dodge, her husband started the truck and revved the engine. The perfectly running engine sent goose bumps all throughout Camara's body. "Something else we have in common."

Chase looked at her, puzzled. She pointed at his hands and legs. "You shake before a race, too."

Chase smiled at her. "What can I say? Adrenaline rush."

Camara nodded her agreement. She knew the feeling only too well.

John raised the flag and dropped it.

Chase gunned the engine. Excitement coursed through Camara's veins as they dropped into the mud pit. Goose bumps rose on her flesh as Camara watched Chase's biceps bulge under the strain of keeping the truck inside the pit. She smiled as she thought about how many times those strong arms had held her and how many times they would hold her in the years to come. Quick as a flash, up and out of the pit they flew.

Erik rushed to their window and gave them their time: 7.46. Chase's smile matched her own. They had just broken both of their own records at Swamper Speedway. Together their combined skills and expertise had paid off. Their new Dodge truck, X-Rivals Domination, truly dominated in both speed and power.

As fast as her fingers would allow, Camara unlatched her harness; then in two long scoots, she slid over to Chase's side.

In the privacy of their mud-encased truck, they wrapped their arms around each other and sealed their rivalry's end with a long, passionate kiss.

ABOUT THE AUTHOR

Debra Ullrick is married to her real-life hero of thirty-four years. She has one grown daughter who is married to a wonderful man. Debra and her husband lived and worked on cow-calf ranches in the Colorado Mountains for over twenty-five years. Recently, they moved to the flatlands. Mud-bog racing, classic cars, monster trucks, writing, reading, drawing western art, watching Jane Austen movies, feeding wild birds, and playing with her Manx cat occupies most of Debra's time. Plus, she loves to hear from her readers. You can email her at christianromancewriter@gmail.com. To check out Debra's other books, visit her Web site at www.DebraUllrick.com.